Friends
&
Fauxs

Friends & Fauxs

Tracie
Howard

BROADWAY BOOKS
New York

Published in the United States by Broadway Books,
an imprint of The Crown Publishing Group,
a division of Random House, Inc., New York.
www.broadwaybooks.com

BROADWAY BOOKS and the Broadway Books colophon
are trademarks of Random House, Inc.

Book design by Donna Sinisgalli

Library of Congress Cataloging-in-Publication Data
Howard, Tracie.
    Friends & fauxs / by Tracie Howard. — 1st ed.
        p.   cm.
    1. Mothers and daughters—Fiction. 2. Actresses—
Fiction. 3. Revenge—Fiction. 4. Man-woman
relationships—Fiction. I. Title. II. Title: Friends and fauxs.
    PS3608.O94F75 2009
    813'.6—dc22

                                    2009000532

ISBN 978-0-7679-2993-6

PRINTED IN THE UNITED STATES OF AMERICA

10 9 8 7 6 5 4 3 2 1

First Edition

This book is dedicated to my friends, who are thankfully not the least bit faux! Though you cannot pick your family (thankfully, I've been tremendously blessed with mine!), you can pick your friends, and I've had the great fortune to have loved ones from New York to Atlanta and all the way to Africa who sustain me and make my life richer in good times, as well as in those times that are more trying.

Acknowledgments

Writing can sometimes be a very lonely profession. In fact, I've been accused of disappearing like a ghost during times when I am at my most prolific, only to resurface later, innocently asking "Hey, where's the party?!" to the confusion and irritation of friends and family alike.

For tolerating this odd behavior, I'd like to first of all thank and acknowledge my husband, Scott Folks, who bears with me during those months of insanity, when I become possessed by these characters and *obsessed* with their lives. (I also tend to have bizarre sleep habits when I'm writing, but we won't go there ☺!) I'd also like to thank my family for their unconditional, unwavering, and never-ending support, including my mom, Gloria Freeman, my sisters, Jennifer Freeman and Alison Howard, my brother-in-law, Donny Smith, my mother-in-law, Margaret Mroz, my nieces, Chelsae Smith and Korian Young, my aunts, Opal and Maryland, as well as all of my wonderful cousins and in-laws.

When I became an author, my favorite daydream was to write all winter (since I abhor cold weather) and to travel and play golf all summer. Though I don't have the formula down quite yet, Scott and I have had many memorable trips with some of our closest friends, all of whom are my *favorite* real-life characters, including Karen and Oswald Morgan (restaurateurs extraordinaire), Sharon Bowen and Larry Morse (thanks for all of the great wine tours in Cape Town), Edbert and Lorri Morales (thanks for your sanity after the cat burglar in the south of France), Pam and Monroe Bowden (the voices of reason), Alicia and Danny Bythewood (Yum! You guys always have the best champagne!), Vikki Palmer (she of the golden spirit), Juan and Judith Montier (Juan for always feeding us gourmet dishes and Judith for always reading the early and rough drafts of my manuscripts!), April and Ted Phillips (for your style and substance), Mario Rinaldi (bon vivant of Paul Goerg Champagne—need I say more!), Vanessa and Bill Johnson (a wonderful couple), and Heidi Malesah (and her two gorgeous sons).

I'd also like to thank Baidy Agne, Oumar Sow, CoAnne Wilshire, and Imara Canady for providing me with friendship and inspiration throughout the years. Additionally, I must thank Rod Edmonds, a lawyer, physician, and friend who helped me with the medical nuances in *Friends & Fauxs*.

Now, down to business! Denise Brown, who is my friend first, and attorney and agent always, is the best, and I thank her for always looking out. I also thank and miss Janet Hill for all that she's done for publishing throughout her career, and more specifically, the guidance that she's given me throughout mine. I'd also like to thank my new editor, Christine Pride, who stepped into this project without missing a beat. And Carol Mackey at Black Expressions is a jewel for representing and promoting African American literature in such a compelling fashion. I thank her for that and for her friendship and support of my work.

I'm also inspired by fellow authors E. Lynn Harris, Eric Jerome Dickey, Nina Foxx, and many others who share their talent and give us all another rich slice of life.

Most supremely, I thank God for making it possible for me to do that which I love, and for giving me life, health, hope, and the love of family and friends.

Friends
&
Fauxs

Chapter 1

M*idas Touch*, Brandon's imposing 191-foot yacht, floated serenely in spite of the churn of afternoon waves that lapped seductively at Saint-Tropez's sandy coastline. He'd recently taken possession of the decadent—even by yachting standards—vessel after spending over a year and tens of millions of dollars working with the best craftsmen in the world on every detail, from the design of the heliport and assortment of smaller boats beneath, to the eighteen-carat gold fixtures that accented the Italian marble in the exquisitely appointed master spa. These extravagant touches were *after* parting with a cool two hundred million for the custom-designed luxury craft itself. Nonetheless, the sight of his equally exquisite wife, Gillian, as she sunned topless on the upper deck made this pricey investment well worth every single euro.

The boat and the beauty, Brandon's two prized possessions, validated that he had successfully outrun the squalor of Mississippi's projects. He'd recently sold his money-minting boutique record label, Sound Entertainment, to one of the major labels for over half a billion dollars; more than enough money to scrub away any lingering stench from the gangster rap game and replace it with the sweet smell of success. He was untouchable. The "S" on Brandon's chest was accented with two vertical slashes right down its middle.

"You are more beautiful every day," he whispered in awe. At the moment, he was speaking of Gillian, rather than the magnificent boat.

"Thanks, darling," Gillian murmured. Her four-carat, flawless diamond stud earrings radiated beneath the Mediterranean sun, which even mid-December was grade-E brilliant.

Brandon could hardly believe that this stunning, exotic creature was all his. The ghetto bumpkin who hadn't known a salad fork from a pair of nose clippers had managed to snag the most beautiful and desired woman in Hollywood, if not the world. Brandon may have been born into dire poverty, without a glint of sophistication, but he applied tenacity and street smarts to build a vast music empire, and then smoothly leveraged that success to pry his way into the film industry. He then used his access to lure Gillian into his grasp, making her a superstar actress and his wife in the process. By far, the latter was her most demanding role to date.

When they met she was a former runway model/struggling actress, but he'd astutely appraised the dazzling diamond that shone unseen beneath the rough. Brandon recognized a star in the making when he saw one, and the woman he met that day sat at the center of her own constellation.

Gillian was simply the most elegant woman he'd ever met. Her poise, beauty, and stature stubbornly defied the fact that she had no money, no career prospects, and no man. And unlike most women, the latter of the list was the least of her concerns.

"Why don't you come in, we wouldn't want any sunburn on that beautiful skin of yours."

"I'll be fine," she said.

"What time is it?" she mumbled, turning away from him. Though there was a slight autumn chill in the air, in the middle of the Mediterranean the still-intense sun felt good against her skin. This was their last outing on the floating palace until next summer, and she wanted to soak up every second of it.

"I'm sure what you really want to know is what time is it in L.A.?" He grinned. "It's four forty-five a.m.," he answered, not needing to consult the hundred-thousand-dollar Chopard timepiece that sat depreciating on his wrist. Today was monumental for both of them.

"That's not what I meant," Gillian insisted. Her posture was relaxed, even languid, though she had every reason to be excited and anxious at the prospect of what the day could bring. Regardless, she felt a chill that had less to do with autumn on the Mediterranean Sea than it did with the fact that she couldn't shake the mist of foreboding that haunted her.

Brandon assumed that her edginess was a case of game-day jitters. These next nine hundred seconds could change her life forever, not to mention his, which was something he'd strived to do since his first car trip across the Mississippi state line.

"I've asked Henri to serve lunch in the media room. Why don't you meet me there in fifteen minutes?" he asked.

"I'm not hungry," she replied. Gillian simply couldn't stomach the thought of sitting anxiously in front of a TV screen passively awaiting news of her fate. She'd much rather lie still, preparing herself for the drama that was sure to unfold in her life, one way or the other. She had no idea how accurate her premonition was.

Brandon smiled and ran his fingers affectionately through her tangle of golden brown hair. "See you shortly, baby," he said, possessively patting her bottom before taking the outer stairs down a level to a state-of-the-art media room, which rivaled any on land or sea.

"Champagne, sir?" the uniformed waiter asked, greeting Brandon the minute he slid his feet into a waiting pair of Hermès slippers. Henri, Brandon's butler, who supervised the impressive collection in the ship's wine cellar, chose a Paul Goerg Rosé Champagne to accompany their lunch of Mediterranean sea bass, which was delivered aboard within an hour of being reeled from the azure blue waters. A sumptuous salade niçoise and freshly baked croissants accompanied it.

Brandon accepted a perfectly chilled glass of the effervescent bubbles and felt similarly buoyed. Though the official announcement had yet to be made, every instinct told him that a big celebration would soon be in order.

High on life, he ordered, "Henri, go down to the wine cellar and bring up our best bottle of Champagne. The most expensive."

"Sir, we have a bottle of Clos du Mesnil Krug 1995 on-board, as well," Henri offered. Though many bottles were more well known, this was an amazing bottle.

"I've never heard of it," Brandon said, dismissively, as if name recognition mattered at all when it came to quality. For him it did, particularly since Brandon's uncultivated palate couldn't distinguish the difference between a sparkling white wine from Napa, and a single-vintage Champagne from the noted region in France.

He settled into one of the butter-soft leather chaises in his state-of-the-art screening room. A custom-designed sur-round sound system was embedded in each chair's headrest allowing the viewer to tailor his audio experience. Snug as a bug in a cashmere rug, he turned to ABC's U.S. West Coast feed. It wasn't long before Demi Moore, Forest Whitaker, and Salma Hayek were announcing the 2009 Oscar nomi-nees. Brandon sat patiently through the names of actors and films, waiting to hear the names of the nominees for Best Actress.

"And the nominees for Best Actress are . . ." began For-est. Brandon leaned forward, literally sitting on the edge of his seat.

"Kate Winslet for *The Long Road*, Angelina Jolie for *Never Kiss and Tell*, Gillian Tillman-Russell for *Gold Diggers* . . ."

Brandon didn't hear another word, only the deafening sound of success, mixed with a rush of pure adrenaline that together was sweeter than any orgasm known to man. His wife, muse, and client had just been nominated for an Oscar! He inhaled deeply, his burly chest expanding with pride, as he savored the moment.

On cue, Henri appeared with two chilled Champagne flutes and a serving of beluga caviar and toast points. "Shall I pour for two?" he asked.

"Absolutely," Brandon replied, as he watched the finesse with which Henri held the silver tray of glasses atop outstretched fingers, while deftly pouring the bottle with his thumb in its conclave bottom. Brandon briefly thought of trying it later, but just as quickly reasoned not to bother, after all, that was what he paid Henri handsomely for.

With both glasses in hand, Brandon headed to the top deck, careful to leave his slippers inside, per the protocol of yachting. He marveled at how cool Gillian remained under gut-wrenching pressure. He presumed that such composure was the result of never having to question ones station in life. Gillian wasn't born with a silver spoon in her mouth, but Imelda, her globetrotting mother, taught her to be at home anywhere in the world, and with anyone in it. He loved and admired that unconditional confidence. While Brandon wore a tailor-made armor of confidence to cover his barely buried insecurities, her confidence was weightless, and worn without effort.

Brandon wanted to jump, scream, and shout the news of Gillian's Oscar nomination to the whole world, but he managed to contain his enthusiasm, regained his couth, and said, "Honey, I think a toast is in order." The cheesy smile on his face said everything else.

This time Gillian did turn to face him. While the thought of winning an Academy Award was intoxicating, it was also fraught with fear, like that terrifying moment after reaching the top of a dizzying roller coaster ride, when you're temporarily weightless, and frightfully anticipating the sheer drop that lay unavoidably ahead. With visible effort, she pushed all thoughts and fears aside and accepted the Champagne from her husband who stood beaming as though *he'd* just been nominated for an Oscar.

"Here's to my wife, the next Best Actress Academy Award winner." He raised his glass triumphantly, bursting with pride. If only his crew from Mississippi could see him now. He was on top of the world.

"One step at a time," Gillian warned. "A nomination doesn't mean a win." She was petrified by the manic sense of glee that lit up his face. He looked like a fat kid who'd been given a lifetime supply of Krispy Kreme doughnuts.

"Trust me," he insisted. "In this case, it does."

Since the day they met to exchange suitcases after a baggage mix-up at LAX, Brandon had been ready and willing to give Gillian the world. After watching her gold-digging mother barter her body and soul for money and power, Gillian had been adamant about not following in those well-heeled footsteps. Before they were married, Gillian got a peak behind the curtains of Brandon's magical kingdom and knew the high price to be paid for the realization of her dreams. Though initially she'd valiantly fought the temptation to accept it all, Brandon had been patient, and had slowly walked her down that slippery slope.

Now that she was perhaps a red carpet away from the culmination of her dreams, Gillian still felt as if she had yet to get her bearings. Things that once seemed so black and white were now varying shades of gray. Aside from being considered, by some, a gold digger, what bothered her more was wondering how complicit she was in her husband's criminal activities? A lost zip drive containing a double set of accounting books recovered from Paulette's belongings told her that at best Brandon was a money launderer. Instead of turning it over to the investigating authorities, she accepted his marriage proposal, right along with the career that she'd so desperately wanted.

But a little money laundering wasn't what caused Gillian sleepless nights; it was the real possibility that Brandon might have been the one who'd cut Paulette's brake line. Her car was parked in his garage, and worst of all, she also had proof that Paulette had been blackmailing Brandon, since she, too, had seen the double set of accounting books. Had Paulette gone to the authorities, Brandon would have lost it all; the stately mansion, the sexy yacht, the collection of cars, Gillian, the butler and the driver, and most importantly, the veneer of respect that he'd craved since he'd scraped the Mississippi mud from the bottom of his boots. Blinded by the lights, cameras, and action of the film career that beckoned just beyond her fingertips, Gillian chose to ignore this possibility. She only prayed that she'd never have to pull the trigger on the smoking gun that now sat locked and loaded. "Madam, there's a phone call for you from a Baroness von Glich," one of the yacht's stewards said, offering her a portable phone.

Gillian took another sip, bracing for the conversation to follow. "Hello?"

"For an Academy Award–nominated actress, that's certainly a boring greeting."

"I'll leave the off-camera drama to you," Gillian rebutted. Only a hint of humor colored her response.

In spite of that, her mother laughed her throaty, Betty Davis laugh. "Casting issues aside, congratulations, my dear. I couldn't be more proud of you." Before Gillian could say "Thank you," Imelda plowed ahead. "After all of the sacrifices I've made, our hard work has finally paid off."

Somehow, Gillian wasn't the least bit surprised that her moment had so quickly become all about her mother. The woman had an uncanny ability to suck the air out of a room, even via long distance and on the open seas. "I haven't won anything yet, so let's not get carried away."

"That's just the point, my dear. This *is* only the beginning. The real work lies ahead of us."

Gillian noted the "us." "I'm sure things will work out just fine," Gillian ad libbed, trying desperately to redirect the course of the conversation.

"Just to be on the safe side, I'll be going back to the States with you and Brandon."

"But, mother—"

"In fact I'm in Nice now and will meet you on the boat in Saint-Tropez this time tomorrow."

By now, Gillian was sitting up straight. After wrapping a grueling publicity tour for *Gold Diggers,* she was physically exhausted and mentally drained. "Brandon and I were planning to be alone," she said, hoping that her mother *might* get the drift. But, of course, it sailed right by her.

"That's nice, honey. But I'm sure that handsome and charming husband of yours won't mind your mother being onboard. After all, that floating mansion of his has six suites, a gym, a gourmet kitchen, living room, formal dining room, a den, and a staff of seventeen." Imelda ticked off the amenities as though she were reading from a sales brochure, so completely did they impress her. "So you'll hardly know I'm there."

That was highly unlikely, Gillian thought, as she prepared to brace herself for the seismic shift her life was sure to take; all because of a little gold statue called Oscar.

Chapter 2

Meanwhile, back in La-La Land, Lydia Patterson was also celebrating. Upon hearing Gillian's name called, the publicist leapt from her couch like a lit firecracker, yelped like a small dog, and then did the cabbage-patch all over her one-bedroom apartment. Visions of Oscar appearances and international press conferences danced through her head. Lydia was so happy that her cheeks soon began to ache from smiling so hard. Finally, after slaving away at ICP Publicity for dried peanuts, she was being validated, and she expected all of the ass-kissing accolades and commensurate pay that should come as a result. After exhausting herself completely, she plopped down on the couch and began to exhaust her trusty Rolodex, making a slew of phone calls to make sure that everyone who mattered knew that *she* was Gillian Russell's publicist. The way she gloated, one would have imagined that if it weren't for *her* alone, Gillian's Oscar nomination would be but a distant and foggy dream.

After wrapping up her calls to an array of family,

friends, *and* fauxs, Lydia picked up the phone again to make the call that really mattered: to her boss. "Keith, it's Lydia," she chirped. She was propped up on the sofa by her rapidly inflating ego and a hefty cushion of self-righteousness. She was on top of the world; ICP would finally stop treating her like a glorified secretary-cum-babysitter and give a diva the respect she deserved.

"What's up?" her boss asked, brusquely. She pictured him on his cell phone languishing in the never-ending 405 traffic jam, trapped in his blue-black Mercedes convertible, slowly creeping from his mini-mansion in the Valley into L.A. The pricey sports car had probably never even met third gear.

"Don't pretend you don't know," she jested. Even though it was only 7:30 a.m., he'd be the only executive in Hollywood who wasn't already buzzing about the Oscar nominations. Today was the day that studios, actors, actresses, and those in "The Business" worked for all year. "Gillian Russell? Oscar nomination?" Duh?

"Of course I know that our client received an Oscar nomination." He sounded annoyed that she'd called and interrupted his slow crawl to work.

"You mean *my* client." She loathed the way a C-list client was "hers," but the second there's a glimmer of success, the same client suddenly became "theirs."

Keith sighed as though he were being forced, at gunpoint, to deal with an unreasonable eight-year-old child. "We all realize that you are the primary publicist on Gillian's account, but let's be clear, she's the company's client. Not yours."

His arrogant, condescending tone really pissed her off. When Lydia initially brought Gillian to the agency, they weren't the least bit interested in an unknown black girl without super-light skin, extra-long hair, or a hefty boob job. It was Lydia, and Lydia alone, who'd fought for the actress. "If it weren't for me, Gillian wouldn't even *be* at the firm," she reminded him.

"Now, Lydia, we've *all* brought in clients. That's what we're hired to do."

Though she didn't like his tone, she bit her tongue and swallowed her pride, at least for now, but once she was walking red carpets around the world with her client it would be on!

"Speaking of clients," he continued, "where is Gillian? We need to schedule a press strategy meeting ASAP. Being nominated is one thing, but winning is quite another, and the right press build-up is critical."

"She and Brandon are yachting the Riviera," she answered off-handedly. She was already imagining her outfit for the Oscars.

"When does she return?"

"I'm not sure," Lydia admitted.

"Well, I strongly suggest that you find out. For all you know, they could be schmoozing with ICM, and you know none of these agencies are above poaching an Oscar-nominated client."

Gillian and Brandon had made it pretty clear that this was their downtime and that they didn't want to be disturbed. But that was before the Oscar nomination. "I'll get right on it," she said, suddenly worried. She'd worked too hard to let someone else cash her lottery ticket.

Chapter 3

Reese Nolan sat in a dazed stupor staring openmouthed at her fifty-inch plasma screen TV, just barely comprehending the fact that her good friend Gillian Tillman had just been nominated for an Oscar. Not a Soul Train, BET, or Essence Award, but a damned Oscar! Perhaps familiarity did breed contempt, because, even though Gillian *was* beautiful and *did* have some talent, as far as Reese was concerned, the girl wasn't *that* good. She didn't know whether to be happy for Gillian, or to simply curl up and cry for herself, and for the good ole days before Paulette's untimely death.

Reese, Gillian, Paulette, and Lauren had been the perennial "It" girls in Manhattan. Reese missed those carefree days of partying like rock stars, being photographed by paparazzi, envied by women, and desired by men. Reese had been the most popular of the foursome: the super-gorgeous, designer-clad wife of NBA superstar Chris Nolan. Lauren was the prima donna, naturally beautiful, trust-fund rich, and always elegant, while Gillian was the bohemian, a successful model with impeccable style and an intoxicating exotic appeal. Then there was Paulette, the mover, shaker, and dealmaker, who made one deal too many, which had led them both to the bottom of that rocky ravine.

Reese's phone blared, halting her bumpy ride down memory lane. Reluctantly, she picked it up. "Hello," she managed.

"Hey, girl. Did you hear the news?" It was Lauren, sounding like a hummingbird high on happy juice. Lauren was one of those lucky people seemingly forever dipped in gold.

There was no use pretending not to know. By now, everyone in Hollywood did. "Yes, and I can't believe it," Reese said, trying to infuse a little enthusiasm into her own voice.

"I am so happy I could scream!" Lauren sounded as if *she* had been nominated. Reese supposed that it was much easier to be genuinely happy for other people when your own world resembled a heaping bowl of cherries.

"Me, too," Reese said. She chided herself for hating and tried to remember that she was lucky to be alive, have financial—if not emotional—security, and most importantly, to have her son.

"I have to get to L.A. right away so we can celebrate."

"That sounds good." Even though Reese wasn't in the mood for a celebration, getting together with Gillian and Lauren did sound like a good idea. They hadn't done that since Paulette's death two years ago. Maybe it would bring some long-awaited closure for them all. But on the other hand, it was Lauren's grand idea to get together for Paulette's baby shower that had been the catalyst for the tragic accident.

It was just like Lauren, Reese thought, to insist on planning a shower, even though Paulette was unmarried, and wasn't telling anyone who the father was. Regrettably, she didn't have to. The fact that Reese had blurted it out after a few too many glasses of Champagne would haunt her forever. She vividly remembered the vicious argument that ensued. Sweet little Lauren went straight for the jugular, viciously ripping open painful family wounds, sending Paulette running hysterically from Brandon and Gillian's house. Reese could close her eyes and see Paulette jump into the driver's seat blinded by tears, and, as if from afar, she saw herself jump in along with her. Sometimes the rest would come to her in the form of a waking nightmare: Mulholland Drive twisting and turning, Paulette losing control of the car, and that terrifying plunge over the edge in a fit of twisted metal, deafening impact, and rocky, wooded terrain. The rest was both history and celebrity folklore.

Unconsciously, Reese ran her finger along the barely visible but jagged line that trekked across her left cheek; an unwanted souvenir that even her hard-fought millions and Hollywood's best plastic surgeons couldn't erase.

"Gotta run," Lauren chirped, "Gideon and I have a sunset to catch."

"Where are you, by the way?"

"We're in Cape Town, leaving for Paris in the morning."

Lauren made it sound as if they were hopping the subway from Soho to Midtown.

Great, Reese thought. Gillian was chilling on her husband's monster yacht on the French Riviera, and Lauren was jetting around the world with her hunky photographer boyfriend, and here she was lying in bed alone in L.A. How pathetic. This was certainly not the life she'd envisioned while plotting, planning, and scheming her way from Queens to Beverly Hills.

Still, things could be much worse, she realized. After all, she did manage to wrangle a handsome fifteen-million-dollar divorce settlement from Chris, in addition to thirty-five thousand dollars a month in child support. After buying and decorating her ten-million-dollar house in Bel Air and investing most of the rest with a financial planner, she used the more than generous child support to cover all monthly expenditures; after all, what seven-year-old needed thirty-five thousand dollars a month? Luckily Chris was good about not questioning how she spent the money.

"Mommy, do I have to go to school today?" asked Rowe, who had climbed into Reese's lap.

"Of course you do. Don't you still want to grow up to be a fireman?"

The cute little boy nodded, solemnly. He was tall for his age and very athletic, just like his father.

"Well, firemen have to be smart so they can figure out how to fight those nasty fires and drive that big red truck." Reese tussled his hair and lightly pinched his cheeks.

"But I don't feel good," he pouted. He laid his head on her chest.

Was this a ploy to avoid school and hang out with her for the day, or was he really not feeling good? Reese wondered. For the last few days he had seemed tired, and his normally toast-colored complexion did seem a little sallow, but when she felt his forehead, there was no sign of a fever.

"I'll tell you what. If you go to school, we'll stop for ice cream when I pick you up after soccer practice. How's that?" Normally, he wouldn't dream of missing soccer practice. He was the team's star, and Reese loved watching her little man run up and down the field with such confidence and ability, again, just like his father.

At the mention of ice cream he brightened a little. "Okay," he reluctantly relented, and then trudged off to his room to get ready for school.

Reese picked up the remote and changed the channel, wishing that she could change her life as easily.

Chapter 4

The land of movie stars, Botoxed brows, and fancy cars was worlds away from the natural beauty of Cape Town, South Africa, a magical place where time stood still once the sun began its seductive descent into the depths of the Atlantic Ocean. Vibrant strobes of color unimagined by Pantone, and vivid streaks of light that Van Gogh could have never dared to create, converged to make each sunset a magnificent one-of-a-kind masterpiece.

Sweet sighs of contentment eased past Lauren's lips, as did Gideon's teasing kisses. The word *blissful* came to her mind. That, Lauren realized, was the best way to describe her post-Paulette life with Gideon, at least most of the time. The two lovers had traveled the world, establishing an easy and fluid bohemian existence, far and away from Lauren's controlling mother, Mildred, her scheming ex-husband, Max, and her own troubling demons, which still clung to her like an odorless vapor, proving that it was much easier to evade flesh and blood than to escape your own haunted thoughts and regret-filled dreams.

Not a day went by that Lauren didn't think of her cousin Paulette and her own involvement in Paulette's death, however tangential. True, there was plenty of blame to go around for the devastating car crash that took Paulette's life and that of her unborn child, beginning with Lauren's sleazy ex-husband, who'd been carrying on a torrid affair with Paulette and was the father of her bastard child. Lauren's last words to her ill-fated cousin were nasty, bitter missives, fired off after discovering the affair and the paternity of the expected child, whose very shower was the inauspicious occasion at which this fight occurred. A shower that had been organized and paid for by Lauren herself!

When she could stomach the count, Lauren realized that her first mistake was marrying Maximillian Neuman III. She allowed her mother to call the shots when it came to choosing and marrying her own husband, just as she'd let her call the shots for most of her life. After careful scrutiny, Mildred selected Max to be her lawfully wed son-in-law because he fit the profile that she'd created: he was tall, light, and handsome; he had an Ivy League education and was an up-and-coming lawyer who was quickly making a name for himself in the right Manhattan legal and social circles. Ideally, she would have preferred for him to have family pedigree, but fortunately the Baines-Reynolds family had plenty of that to go around, since they boasted four generations of wealth, position, and the right complexion; though, these days, the last counted for far less. In any case, Mildred had led Lauren down the aisle like a little lamb to slaughter.

Lauren's second regret was not being sensitive to the insidious family politics surrounding skin color that had begun generations ago, when her great-great-grandmother, after being raped by the slave master, saw the high yellow baby appear between her black-as-coal legs, and instantly saw her ticket to the promised land. And so it was. The master freed her and the baby and even freed her other black children and her husband. He didn't stop there, either; he educated them all and thus began the steep climb of the Baines dynasty. From then on they married only other "similarly situated" blacks, so when Priscilla, Lauren's grandmother, had Mildred and Paulette's mother, June, and June emerged from between her snowy white thighs the color of soot, a legacy of favoritism and rivalry was born right along with her.

During their senior year of high school, to add insult to injury, June, who was the darker and hence less-favored Baines daughter, somehow managed to lure the judge's son, who had already been earmarked for Mildred, into her clutches. This was an unforgivable breach of hierarchy that tore asunder any closeness the two sisters had shared. Disgraced, June ran off with a common day worker and was promptly disowned. She returned nine months later with Paulette, who'd suffered the wrath of color discrimination, snobbery, and bad breeding ever since.

While June bore her cross silently, Paulette meticulously harbored and nurtured deep resentment toward Mildred that by default spilled over onto the picture-perfect Lauren. Her resentment and insecurities were unintentionally fed and fertilized by Mildred, who never let Paulette forget that she was a resident of the *other* side of the family tracks.

Lauren, on the other hand, played it safe, and kept her well-coiffed head buried in the sand, feigning oblivion to the insidious family politics that ate away at her cousin, and fool-hardily believed that she could pretend it didn't exist and that she therefore would not have to deal with it.

While sleeping dogs may lie, and some may never kiss and tell, revenge *is* best served cold, all of which Lauren soon discovered. When Lauren found out about Paulette and Max's affair and the pregnancy, the two women fought bitterly; it was an explosive argument that resulted in Paulette's tearful and hysterical drive down the Hollywood Hills, made tragic by a cut brake line, as well as the cutthroat curves of Mulholland Drive.

Lauren's guilt was immense. Shortly after the funeral she left the country with Gideon and had not once looked back.

"A penny for your thoughts," Gideon whispered, in between the trail of kisses he eased along her throat, while stroking her hair and holding her close.

She could feel him swelling against her thigh; a knowing smile courted the edges of her lips. "Haven't you heard? The dollar is worthless; I'm not even sure if the penny even still exists," she teased.

He rolled over onto one side and dug deep into his cargo pants, extracting a rand, South Africa's currency. "Okay, what about a rand?"

"Last time I checked it was seven to one on the dollar. Totally not worth the price of my thoughts."

"Okay, what about a kiss. I mean a *real* kiss," he said, as he rolled back above her, pinning Lauren with his piercing gaze.

"Now you're talking," Lauren cooed, squirming invitingly beneath him. Their connection, as it had been since they met, was impenetrable.

Their lips met as though they had been handcrafted to fit snugly together, and the way they licked, sucked, and devoured each other was a fait accompli. Lauren loved his weight on top of her as they kissed and the contours of his well-cut muscles against her softness. Best of all, she savored the heat that radiated from the throbbing length of muscle between his legs. Gideon never failed to make her pant, which eased her legs open in invitation. No RSVP was ever required.

Gideon pulled away, leaving her breathless. "What's on my baby's mind?"

"Nothing that can't wait," she said, as she pulled at his zipper, ready to get the party started.

"We've got the rest of our lives. I just want to hear that you're happy, that's all."

"If I were any happier, I'd explode."

"That's exactly what I was waiting to hear."

After removing the rest of her clothes, he covered her body in soft wet kisses, lingering on her taut nipples, licking, teething, and sucking them until lazily trading one for the other. Meanwhile his hand traveled south, to a tropical land that he knew all too well. As his fingers probed and explored, Lauren moistened and massaged them with her muscles, communicating to him in a language that he understood instinctively. Gideon answered her plea by easing his thickness between her legs, conquering her wetlands.

They made love, hungrily, giving it good, and getting it even better. Nothing was held back. Flipping over, Lauren rode him until she felt the tightness that always preceded her orgasm. It lingered in her groin for a while, then did a teasing radiant dance that spread the magic through, down, and around her hot sex. She closed her eyes and saw vibrant strobes of color and vivid streaks of light. Then she heard deep moans, primal groans, and unintelligible sounds that all came together in a soaring duet. Lauren and Gideon held on to each other as the sun completed its seductive descent into the depths of the ocean.

Blissful, yeah, that's what it was, blissful. Lauren eased into unconsciousness with a smile on her face, and just a whisper of unease hovering overhead.

Chapter 5

Imelda swept aboard the *Midas Touch* with two steamer trunks in tow, wearing a black, oversized floppy hat, a bright Zac Posen shift, handcrafted, crystal-studded stilettos, and a pair of humongous black sunglasses, the kind that celebrities wore when they wanted to be seen not being seen.

"Brandon, you look amazing!" she lied, effusively kissing the air near his pudgy cheeks three times, back and forth. "I love a man with a big, long—boat," she teased, before turning her attention to Gillian. "Oh, darling, I am sooooo proud of you."

Midsentence she was already scanning the opulent surroundings. Gillian wasn't sure whether her mother's pride was related to her Oscar nomination or her apparently inherited ability to marry a rich man. "Thanks, Mom," Gillian managed through a tight smile.

"You know, dear," Imelda started, absently lifting the glass of Champagne offered by Henri, "I've been thinking about the intense media scrutiny that we will soon be under." Imelda spoke as though she were a costar nominated right alongside her daughter. She took a distressed breath, dramatizing the gravity of the statement to come. "The mom thing . . ." she began, shaking her head before lowering it as though trying hard to comprehend the complex issue that was weighing heavily on her mind. "I think it's best that you call me Imelda from now on, especially in public."

"Mom!" Gillian was genuinely surprised, but not utterly shocked. She knew her mother all too well.

"Just a thought," Imelda offered in wide-eyed earnestness. "I was only thinking of you, darling. I wouldn't want people to think you have a stage mom lurking around."

Imelda was actually thinking about being center stage herself, out in front of the world audience, which included thousands of possible ex-husbands in the making, and damned if she wanted to be cast as a mom. There was nothing sexy about that. In fact, the way she saw things, she and Gillian looked more like sisters anyway.

Sensing the tension between the two women, this seemed as good a time as any for Brandon to manage an exit. "Henri, would you get the porters to direct the Baroness to her quarters?" He turned to Gillian and Imelda, who were facing off like two ornery cats in a dark back alley. "I have some work to do. I'll see you at dinner, seven-thirty."

Imelda took the opportunity to escape as well. She'd revisit the mom thing another time. "We'll talk later," she promised her daughter before following Henri and the porters to her spacious, luxuriously appointed stateroom.

Later, sprawled chin-deep in a milky bubble bath, which she had one of the staff draw, Imelda's mind raced with the intoxicating possibilities offered by Gillian's new status and Brandon's hefty loads of money. She'd known that Brandon had money when he and Gillian were dating—his Beverly Hills house and fleet of cars advertised that fact—but she didn't realize that he had *real* money. Buying a custom yacht was not for the faint of wallet. She quietly praised her daughter for having the good sense to marry the man, as unappealing as he was. After all, marrying a mere millionaire was hardly enough these days. Hell, it probably cost a million a year just to service this floating paradise, she thought, looking around at the imported tile, solid gold fixtures, and state-of-the-art entertainment system, even in a guest suite! Not to mention the staff of seventeen that included two drivers who met the boat at each port of call with two Mercedes sedans. What a life. It was certainly one that she could, and would, get used to.

Dinner that evening was a candlelit affair in the yacht's main dining room. Henri and his staff of servers set the table with the custom china that Brandon had commissioned Colin Cowie to design. An elaborate "R" crest, meant to convey family legacy, nestled in the center of each piece. As appetizers of fresh tomato bisque and mini herb-crusted lamb chops were served, Imelda poured on years of practiced charm and a large dose of feminine wiles, along with a side of wit.

"When I was in my twenties in Paris I was once approached by Valentino himself on the Champs-Elysées. As flattered as I was—you know I was a beauty—I had to decline his offer to be his muse and model. After all, I was married to my third husband then, and he was a very rich and influential man, so why should I work?" She sighed wistfully. "Though perhaps I should have had a career."

Other than marrying rich men, Gillian thought.

"A career like Gillian's." Imelda gazed at her daughter longingly. Time was a vicious, nasty bitch, she thought. How wholly unfair that her daughter sat casually wearing her beauty without a second thought. She wasn't even wearing a bra, yet her perky young breasts stood up, anxious to be noticed. Without a hint of makeup, her Mediterranean tan lit up the room, nor was there one wrinkle, sag, or shadow lurking beneath her eyes. For sure, Imelda was very well put together for a woman of a certain age, but it wasn't without the aid of Wonderbras, miracle creams, and the occasional nip and tuck.

"So, Baroness, how long will you be visiting with us?" Brandon asked. He loved calling his mother-in-law Baroness. Regardless of the fact that her last ex-husband purchased his title, and that it essentially meant nothing, it nonetheless elevated Brandon's stature merely to be in close proximity to a royal title.

"Oh, I'm not sure. There's nothing for me to rush back to, so I'm prepared to stay as long as necessary."

Her statement, combined with the steamer trunks, spelled trouble to Gillian. It was one thing for her mother to just pop up in France and then invite herself back to the States, but it was another not to offer a departure date.

Besides, she knew that if her mother smelled money and/or power that she would be relentless in her quest for her share, and unfortunately she and Brandon now reeked of both.

"I think we have things under control, so you really don't have to bother coming out to L.A." Gillian tried valiantly to ward off the inevitable, though she knew that her weak effort was for naught.

Imelda was not to be diverted. She placed her knife and fork down and adopted a serious, maternal expression. "Honey, you're going to need all of the support you can get right now, and I'd be less of a mother if I weren't there to help you at this critical time."

Gillian was baffled by the way Imelda was able to give that little speech with a straight face, particularly when only hours ago, she'd asked not to even be called mom. Amid her puzzlement, for the first time in her life, Gillian also felt a tinge of sympathy. There was an air of desperation clinging to her mother that she'd never detected before. She suddenly seemed older and much more vulnerable.

As though sensing this opening, Imelda smoothly played the sympathy card. "Life is short, and I've already missed enough of yours while living abroad. I want to make up for that, and spend whatever time I have left focusing on you." She reached across the table and gently grabbed her daughter's hand in a very touching Oscar-worthy gesture. Before Gillian could react, Imelda sealed the deal. She turned to Brandon with imploring eyes. "Unless of course your handsome husband objects to my being around."

There was no graceful way to object, so Brandon followed Imelda's script. "Of course not. We'd love to have you stay."

"Well, it's settled," Imelda proclaimed, as though Brandon had finally managed to talk *her* into an extended stay. "I'll send for more things once we're back in the States."

Great, Gillian thought, just what I need. Suddenly, that creepy feeling of foreboding was ratcheted up another notch.

Chapter 6

The years since Reese's tragic auto accident had been understandably rough on her, but she counted her many blessings every day, namely the number of zeros included in the balance of her well-endowed investment account, and her equally handsomely funded bank account (courtesy of Chris's more than generous child support payments), not to mention her stately five-bedroom, midcentury estate, which sat nestled in a pristine perch above Beverly Hills. She reigned over her manor like Imelda Marcos lording over her vast collection of shoes.

Situated behind a gated motor court, the classic eleven-and-a-half-million-dollar lair boasted an Olympic-size pool, a luxury cabana, immaculate gardens, and a separate guesthouse. Best of all, for Reese, were the commanding views from the glass-walled open floor plan of Century City, the mountains, and the ocean. Queens, New York, was nowhere in sight.

She'd fought long and hard and sold her soul at a discount to get to where she was. Accident, death, and destruction aside, she would probably do it all over again in order to have the financial security she now enjoyed. Even so, her victory was a somewhat hollow one.

Together she and Paulette had devised a scheme to have Chris followed, and uncovered photographic proof that he was on the down low. They then threatened to expose him, effectively ending his NBA career, if he didn't agree to her outrageous settlement demands, which were far outside of the prenup they'd both signed. Reese got what she wanted: Chris's money. Their cutthroat tactics and his visceral anger were both viable motives for murder, thus Chris was also snared into the net of suspects for Paulette's murder.

Reese's biggest regret was how she'd initially used Rowe. Having a baby had originally only been a tactic to ensure that Chris was safely snared, along with his tens of millions, but at her lowest point, ironically, it had been Rowe's love that sustained her. Aside from Rowe, whose unconditional love was a source of immense comfort, there was very little love in her life. Sure, Gillian and Lauren were both great friends and would be there in a heartbeat if she needed them, but they had their own full lives that otherwise didn't really include her. Her remaining family, her mother and a brother, both only came calling when they needed something, namely, money. And Chris, though he sent his child support faithfully each month, and made every effort to see and be in touch with Rowe (even though they lived a continent apart), wanted nothing to do with Reese. She couldn't really blame him after all that she'd put him through.

Which was why she sat alone overlooking her gardens while having a light lunch. At least she had Gillian's celebration later to look forward to.

"Mrs. Nolan, you have a call," Gretchen, Reese's housekeeper said, as she hustled down the cobblestoned path to where Reese sat sipping a flute of Cristal.

"Take a message." It was probably someone else calling to gloat over Gillian's nomination. Since Gillian's Oscar nomination, Reese must have gotten a zillion calls from so-called friends, fauxs, and simple nosy Nellies all wanting to talk to someone who knew Gillian Tillman-Russell personally, as though the glitz and glamour might rub off on them merely through association. She couldn't take another minute of being reminded of just how fabulous Gillian was, not when she only had to look in the mirror or at the empty pillow next to hers to be reminded of just how *not* fabulous she was.

It certainly wasn't for lack of effort. Over the last year, she'd had multiple plastic surgeries to repair the damage from the car accident; a face-lift in an attempt to pull it all together; a nose job, just because; liposuction to suck away some of the fat that had gathered when she couldn't hit the gym like she used to; breast augmentation; a toe tuck to trim down excess from her left pinky toe (a deal-breaker when sporting Jimmy Choos); and last but not least, vagioplasty to tighten and tone her punany. After all of that she still lacked the magic that she once wielded effortlessly. Regardless, tonight she planned to put her best Manolo forward.

"Ma'am, they say it's an emergency. It's Master Rowe's

school." Gretchen looked embarrassed to insist on having Reese take the call, but like everyone else who came into contact with Rowe, she'd grown extremely close to him over the last three years, and was alarmed by the phone call.

Reese raised her brow, which wasn't so easy given the regularly scheduled injections of Botox, and took the phone; concern took root before she even answered it. The elite Harvard-Westlake private school that Rowe attended never called midday with any sort of emergency. "Hello?"

"Mrs. Nolan, this is Mrs. Owens, the head nurse at Harvard-Westlake, there's been a problem with Rowe and we need you to come right away."

The concern that had taken root seconds before was now in full bloom. "What kind of problem? Where is he?" Reese jumped up from the chair, spilling her glass of wine.

"Please calm down, Mrs. Nolan, Rowe is stable now. He's in the nurse's station, but he probably needs to see a doctor."

"Don't tell me to calm down!" Reese shouted. "What happened to my baby?"

"He went out for recess and suddenly he became short of breath and a bit listless. We immediately brought him into the nurse's station, where he began vomiting. We took his temperature and it was a hundred and one."

"Why didn't someone call me?" Reese demanded.

"This all just happened, and of course our first concern was to make sure that Rowe was stabilized. Now that he is, you should call his pediatrician and head over right away."

Two minutes later Reese was snapping her seat belt into place as she floored her chocolate Aston Martin, spewing pebbles along the driveway. On her panicked drive down the hills of Bel Air she couldn't help but relive those last frantic moments along the mountainous terrain before she and Paulette crashed that fateful night. A sinking feeling settled over her, as she thought of and prayed for Paulette.

Ten minutes later she skidded to a halt in front of the immaculately constructed learning haven for the rich and richer. She raced through the doors in search of her son. After navigating the sprawling school, with the help of a custodian who was very busy polishing the marble floors to the highest shine humanly possible, she located the movie set-ready nurses station.

"Where is he?" Reese demanded from the starched white-clad receptionist. "Rowe Nolan. Where is he?"

Recognizing an out-of-control parent, the receptionist calmly stood up and said in her most soothing voice, "If you'll just have a seat, I'll get the head nurse here right away. It shouldn't take her more than a couple of minutes."

"I don't want a seat, or to see the head nurse, what I want right now is my son!" The polish that lots of green (the monetary type) had buffed to a shine on Reese was all gone. There was nothing left but the scrappy, scruffy, ready-to-rumble little girl from Queens. The one who would sooner fight than look at you twice.

"Mrs. Nolan," another calm voice said, "Rowe is just back here, resting. Follow me."

Reese hiked her Hermès bag higher up on her shoulder and followed the voice that belonged to a heavyset woman with unnaturally orange hair and thighs that rubbed together loudly with each step. They arrived at Rowe's room where he lay with covers up to his chin, the mischievous gleam missing from his big brown eyes.

"Honey," Reese leaned over to whisper, "are you okay?

He shook his head listlessly, as if the effort alone were too much for his small body to bear.

"Tell Mommy where it hurts."

He shrugged his small shoulders and said, "All over."

"We took Nolan's temperature about ten minutes ago and it was one hundred and three. He's unusually listless and lethargic, and seems pale. It could very well be an infection of some kind, but I would strongly recommend that you get him to his pediatrician right away."

It broke Reese's heart to see her son lying there so helpless, her strong, vibrant son who fancied himself the "man of the house." He watched every game his father played, often with a running commentary more specific than any coach or network announcer, and tried to mimic his father's famous moves on his miniature basketball court out back.

An hour later Reese and Rowe were in one of Dr. Young's patient rooms; Reese was as nervous as a whore in church, while little Rowe lay on the examination table barely able to keep his eyes open.

"What seems to be the problem, big guy?" Dr. Young asked, tussling Rowe's tight dark curls. His adorable little face was twisted in pain and his eyes looked like two empty windows to a tired soul.

"I don't feeeeel good." It took the normally loquacious seven-year-old just about all the energy he had to say those four words.

"Well, let's take a look and see if we can figure out what's going on. We can't have our next star forward not feeling good." Dr. Young's well-known bedside manner brought a small smile to Rowe's face, and calmed Reese, as well.

He busied himself taking Rowe's temperature and blood pressure, all the while maintaining an animated one-sided banter about the Eastern versus Western Conference.

When he left the room, he asked Reese to follow. "I'm going to order some routine blood work, a complete blood cell count, and a monospot."

"A mono what?"

"A test to check for mononucleosis."

"Isn't he a little young for that?" Her only frame of reference was that this was the "kissing disease."

"No, it's a virus that he could easily have caught at school, sharing utensils." He paused. "I'm not saying that's what he has; my job is to rule out as many causes as possible, and hone in on the one real problem, and then take care of it."

He motioned for one of his nurses to come over and rattled off a list of instructions to her, while Reese stood by dumbfounded.

"Mrs. Nolan, try not to worry, it could be a simple virus."

"I know, I know. Take two aspirins and call me in the morning."

"Close, but not quite," Dr. Young joked. "I'll have some test results tomorrow morning and *I'll call you*. Until then, I'll give you something for his fever. Tuck him in and make sure that he gets lots of fluids and a good night's rest."

Chapter 7

The sleek black Bentley glided to a stop in front of the red carpet at the W Hotel, L.A.'s hottest hotspot. The velvet ropes were lined with the hip, the famous, and those who desperately craved to be one or the other. Many would still be there hours from now with their noses pressed longingly against the window. L.A. was a ruthless town—definitely not for the socially weak, or the personally humble.

Lydia was as excited as an eight-year-old who'd overdosed on glucose. After spending her mediocre career wet-nursing lackluster B- and C-list celebrities, she had finally landed a bona-fide star, and she planned to ride Gillian's ascent straight to the top. "Don't forget, we'll do a full interview with Shaun Robinson at *Access Hollywood*, followed by brief chats with *Extra* and *USA Today*; everyone else, we'll breeze right by."

At the mere mention of press, attention-hungry Imelda perked right up. "Are you sure that's a good idea? It seems to me that we should get all the press we can." She had been practicing Paris Hilton's "over one shoulder" pose and had it down to camera-ready perfection. With all of those cameras and microphones beckoning, this little twit was telling her to ignore them. Was she crazy?

The "we" part did not go unnoticed by Lydia. "At this point I don't want Gillian overexposed," she patiently explained. "She needs to maintain the same air of mystery that's worked so well for her."

"That was before, but now we're talking about an Academy Award and worldwide press," Imelda announced, as if this had somehow escaped everyone else's attention.

The last thing Lydia needed was a meddling, has-been mother trying to weasel her way into the spotlight. It was bad enough having to deal with the stage moms of teenage celebrities, but she could see that dealing with a well-seasoned cougar like Imelda made dealing with those women a walk in the park by comparison. Imelda only cared about Gillian's career to the extent that it furthered her own cause.

"This strategy has been well thought out," Lydia replied with a glint of steel in her voice. "We want the Academy and the fans to always be left wanting more of Gillian, not feeling as if they've already had enough." The agency had several strategy sessions and decided that this was the best way to go to ensure that Gillian not only brought home the gold statue, but also built a career that had substance and longevity. They'd gone over the plan with Brandon and Gillian, who were both in agreement, so she certainly didn't appreciate being second-guessed by her client's cloying mother.

"I still think it's important that people get to know her," Imelda said, tossing her weave dismissively. She was not one who was easily put off. She suddenly brightened as an idea came to her. "Perhaps, as a surrogate, *I* could talk to the rest of the media on her behalf."

I'm sure you would love that, Lydia thought, barely holding back a smirk. "I don't think that's a good idea," she answered simply, dismissing the subject, just as the driver opened the back curbside door for Gillian.

Lydia said, "Remember, keep a smile on when you're working the red carpet. You have to assume that you're being photographed every single second. And you know photographs show up everywhere these days." Lydia was like a boxing trainer prepping a heavyweight before a big bout as she finished laying out the game plan for Gillian's dramatic entrance.

Gillian emerged from the car to streams of popping flashbulbs, rolling cameras, throngs of reporters, and a line of eager fans, all anxious to catch a glimpse of the actress who'd rocketed from obscurity to fame literally overnight. Her long, tanned legs seemed to go on forever as she stood to her full six-foot height. She wore an Elie Saab couture dress that clung beautifully to her model-size frame.

Lydia slid out next, ready to usher Gillian along the press rope and down the red carpet. Meanwhile, Imelda, who was supposed to exit past the carpet and meet them inside, had glossed her already MAC-covered shiny lips and was sliding over to pop out behind Lydia. Thinking quickly, and not wanting a replay of Gillian's first premiere, where

Imelda had weaseled her way right into interviews and then had the nerve to hog the microphone, Lydia gingerly pushed the door closed behind her, effectively slamming it in Imelda's face. If looks could kill, Imelda's hateful glare would have penetrated the tinted glass window and landed dead center between Lydia's eyes.

After escaping the mother-from-hell, Lydia guided Gillian over to Shaun Robinson from *Access Hollywood*, who was already set up and waiting for the interview.

"Gillian, how does it feel to be nominated for an Oscar?" Shaun asked, as her cameraman pulled in for the requisite close-up.

"I am so honored and tremendously flattered to be nominated along with the other amazing actresses in the category," Gillian beamed. Her smile lit up the night, causing another flurry of flashes to capture the moment.

"What do you think your odds are of winning?"

Gillian chuckled. "Well, I've never been a gambler, so I'm not sure. I can only hope that my work speaks for itself."

"Where is your hubby tonight? He must be so proud of you."

"Yes, he is, and he'll be here a little later." Gillian hated talking about Brandon. She realized that many people believed that he'd bought and paid for her, and her career. She would rather believe that she'd made it based on her talent, though she'd never know since Brandon financed *Gold Diggers*, her first and only film, and poured even more money into her marketing, promotion, and press. His money also bought her a first-rate stylist and a hair and makeup team who were on call 24-7. These were perks that no first-time actress would have dreamed of, unless of course she happened to be sleeping with, or was married to, the financier.

Ever alert, Lydia signaled for Shaun to wrap up the interview. For the same reasons as Gillian, she didn't want any questions about Brandon included in interviews. It was important that Gillian be perceived as a serious actress, not a by-product of the casting couch.

The photographers along the red carpet couldn't get enough of Gillian as she reluctantly posed for a few shots. There was nothing more pathetic than those desperate celebrities who crawled along the red carpet posing with each step until everyone with a disposable camera had taken their picture.

Once inside Gillian was whisked past the B-list celebrities and a cadre of hangers-on who were fortunate enough to know someone who knew someone, and therefore were able to get into the building but weren't well-connected enough to actually make it into the coveted VIP section, which was where the real party would be. The whole scene was sharply ironic to Gillian, who vividly recalled being relegated to C-list status after arriving in L.A. With no connections, she'd barely made it past the front door and was then shunted to an uncool section of the club that was the social equivalent of Alaska. My how things have changed, she thought. Less than two years later, even though she was the exact same person, she was suddenly the reigning queen of Hollywood. Note to self, she thought: Easy come, easy go.

"Congratulations!!" screamed Lauren and Reese. They both stood just inside the VIP room with Champagne glasses in hand, beaming from ear to ear.

The three shared a group hug that was haunted by Paulette's absence. They each had to wrestle their own demons as a result of Paulette's untimely death.

If only Paulette hadn't been so upset by their argument, Lauren lamented; she might have been able to somehow stop the sabotaged Mercedes before it went plummeting over the rugged canyons off of Mulholland Drive. The sad irony was that the egomaniacal Max wasn't worth nearly the high price they'd all paid for the affair. Of course, Mildred, Lauren's socialite-cum-arbiter-of-everything-that-mattered mother, was of the very vocal opinion that her scurrilous niece, Paulette, got *exactly* what she deserved.

As far as Mildred was concerned, it was bad enough that decades earlier Paulette's mother, June, had soiled their illustrious family legacy, but for Paulette to plow even deeper into the gutter by having an affair with her cousin's husband, and then plot to have his child, clearly demonstrated why both mother *and* daughter belonged on the *other* side of the family tracks.

Whenever Reese looked into the mirror—something she used to do much more often—she was instantly reminded that while she escaped the tangled wreckage of the accident broken and battered, Paulette—her partner in crime—lay in a cold dark grave. The physical scars she bore, though no longer angry slashes across her once flawlessly beautiful face, weren't nearly as deep and damaging as the mental scar that no surgeon's scalpel could ever repair. The scars were also reminders that the tragic accident could have been her fault.

Paulette had been a take-no-hostages barracuda when it came to getting what she wanted, so she had no shortage of enemies whose ire she'd stoked and provoked on her rough trek from the wrong side of the tracks to being the owner of one of the hottest PR firms in New York and L.A. The fact that Reese's ex-husband, Chris, was one such victim was due to Reese's own brand of at-all-cost tactics. For years she'd schemed and connived and used every trick in the gold-digger handbook to separate as much of Chris's NBA millions from his wallet as possible. Like a seasoned gold digger, Reese even used her son as leverage. Unfortunately, she'd also used Paulette. In fact, the two women were simpatico; they'd understood each other completely. They were opposite sides of the same rusted coin. While Paulette's self-esteem had long ago been replaced by a pain that she sought to soothe with a steady diet of food, men, money, and material things, Reese had overdosed on self-esteem and had a supersized ego, which required perpetual care and feeding.

"Paulette would have been so proud of you," Reese said, with a tight smile that staved off her tears. Though she'd been hesitant to leave Rowe, she was glad that she had come to celebrate and be with her friends. She'd given Rowe his medicine, tucked him in, and sat at his bedside gently rubbing his head until he fell asleep, just the way he had done for her when she was in the hospital after the accident.

"I know. If it weren't for Paulette, I wouldn't even be

here," Gillian said. Though famous for her cool (and beauty), she had her own demons to deal with. The source of her guilt and pain was unspeakable, and nearly unthinkable. She hadn't told anyone of her suspicions that Brandon had a strong motive for murdering Paulette.

She'd believed Brandon when he'd insisted that he had not laundered drug money through Sound Entertainment but was being set up. It was much more convenient to believe that those glorious millions he spent on her were legitimate than to kiss them all good-bye. When confronted with the truth, Gillian still clung to those millions rather than risk wrecking her gravy train. She hid the flash drive and never said a word to anyone, including Brandon. She buried her friend, along with the truth, and then married the man and his money.

"Here's to the success of *Gold Diggers*," Lauren said, meaning the film, though in Gillian's heart she realized that though she had felt morally superior to Reese and Paulette, often calling them gold diggers, a character trait she'd learned to abhor after watching her mother slither from one wealthy man to another, it was quite possible that she was the biggest gold digger of them all.

Chapter 8

It never failed to amaze Charli how base and predictable most men were. They responded to stimuli as loyally as Pavlov's well-trained dogs did to the dinner bell, she mused, while turning her back to a group of middle-aged men and flawlessly executing the Booty Shake, a stripper's move that put Atlanta and the renowned club Stripper's Joint on the map. It was considered the money move because the sight of a woman's well-endowed buttocks rotating rhythmically to the beat of *anything* drove the human male species primally insane and, in the case of her customers, it also drove the money right out of their pockets. The gazed, fixed, partially open eyes, nearly drooling mouth, and the wide-open wallet were all familiar sights to Charli Kemble. She was the premier attraction at the city's most noted strip club. She didn't have the biggest butt—not in a southern city well known for ample, rotund backsides— nor did she have the largest breasts or longest weave, which were other necessary accoutrements for city strippers. What

Charli did have in abundance was an uncanny command of her female wiles and rampant sex appeal. While most of the girls bordered on slutty in their lame and overt attempts to attract men—showing everything they had, in addition to what they'd bought—she took the opposite tack, letting her sexuality only allude to the mind-blowing erotic pleasure that a night with her surely promised.

"That's right, baby, back dat ass up!" one guy moaned, as he slid to the end of his chair nearly salivating. If only his prim and proper wife could have seen her ordinarily conservative, boring husband at that moment, she'd have been on the pole herself!

Charli barely even heard his words of encouragement. She was very good at blocking out the slobbering bozos who sat drooling over her for hours while dispensing their hard-earned money like a well-tapped ATM. Instead, she focused on the large piles of cash that awaited her at the end of each night.

She would never have imagined when she arrived in Atlanta four years ago that she'd be shaking her ass every night in front of total strangers, nor did she imagine that she'd be driving a Porsche 911 and own her own luxury condo downtown. The bad always seemed to come right alongside the good. Good, bad, or indifferent, she wouldn't trade her sometimes-seamy way of life for the small-town existence her mother lived for anything in the world.

Fortunately, her mom, Teresa Kemble, had no idea what Charli *really* did for a living. As far as she knew her daughter was a telemarketing supervisor for a telecommunications

company, and since she never traveled to Atlanta, the hedo-
nistic capital of the south, she never had to wonder how a
low-level employee such as her daughter could drive an
eighty-thousand-dollar car.

"I need you in the VIP room," Flash, the club manager
ordered as Charli shimmied back into her clothes, hundreds
of dollars richer.

"My shift is up," Charli replied without bothering to
look at him. Flash was even slimier than his customers, if
that was possible.

"This ain't no nine-ta-five, shawty. I got some ballers
askin' for you 'specially."

"Not interested." It was 2 a.m. and she'd been shakin'
her ass since eight.

"It's Lil' Easy and his crew, and you know how generous
the rappers are. The last time they was up in here Shaniqua
walked away with at least two grand." Flash waited, knowing that by waving dollar signs, the tide would soon turn his
way. Eventually, a flash of cash worked for all the hos up in
the club. They all started out stripping with some marginal
scruples and a few limits, up until the right amount of
money pushed both aside. He had to admit that, so far,
Charli's threshold was much higher than most. She was
skinny by his standards, but she had something beyond tits
and ass that was irresistible to his customers. If only she
wasn't so difficult, they'd both be richer for it.

But two grand did get her attention. Even though Charli
had a hefty bank account with well over six figures resting in
it, she never felt as if she had enough. There was always a

subconscious sense of doom that clung to her, a feeling that she'd never be prepared for all life might have in store for her.

As much as she wanted to walk out the door and cleanse her mind, body, and soul of the residue from hours of entertaining the sexual fantasies of creepy horny men, an extra couple of thousand dollars for an hour's work did have a certain cleansing quality in itself. How many people made two thousand dollars an hour? That was over thirty-three dollars a minute. All of a sudden, the cover-up that was going over her thong and pasties reversed course and slid off instead.

"Be in VIP One in ten minutes," Flash ordered, barely concealing a smirk. No matter how high and mighty, every ho had her price. For some of the hood rats that'd descended on Atlanta in the last ten years, all chasing rappers and athletes, the price was as low as the cost of tightening up a foot-long weave. Then, of course, there were women like Gillian, who had accurately assessed her assets and priced them accordingly. The next level were those sadly repressed southern belles whose perceived value went far beyond the physical, and included family history, educational achievement, and looks (to a lesser degree). Many of the women of this ilk in the Chocolate City couldn't find their own G spots with a Google Map and a GPS device. They usually sold out for a husband who wore a suit and tie, two bratty kids, and a picket fence in the suburbs.

Charli stopped off in the dancer's green room, which was more puke-green than anything, to freshen up. In dim light the club took on the aura of naughty, high-class decadence, and the girls appeared to be on the exotic side of slutty. But turn on the lights, and the sexy lounge revealed its dingy walls, stained furniture, and cheap carpet. Worse yet, the girl whom men had felt motivated to trade in the wife and kids for, three hundred dollars ago, suddenly looked like a wrung-out addict on her last hit of crack.

Juicy, a hooker who masqueraded as an exotic dancer, strutted through the door, cupping her 38-Ds. "Girrrl, you goin' in the VIP room?" she asked Charli.

"Unfortunately," Charli answered. She kept her dialogue with the other dancers, most of whom resented her unearned popularity with the clients, especially those clients who were more sophisticated and usually had more cash, to a minimum.

"What you mean, unfortunately?" Juicy responded with a well-practiced snap of the neck. "Most of us would kill to be up in there with Lil' Easy and his crew."

Charli knew better than to answer. Juicy and her crew of skanks were always looking for a reason to check her. Charli was ruddy-brown with exotic, chiseled features and light brown hair, which she wore in a pageboy.

Bunny, a ghetto chick from Bankhead, rolled her eyes at Charli and muttered, "Bitch," for no good reason.

After glossing her lips, brushing a bit of powder over her face, and running her fingers through her hair, Charli was quick to escape the hornet's nest. She could feel the sharp daggers in her back as she left the room.

When she and four other dancers walked into the VIP suite, it was set up with bottles of Veuve Clicquot on each table. Lil' Easy and his hangers-on were slouched in their chairs smoking blunts and bobbin' their heads to a remix of Lil' Wayne's *A Milli*. Like a hungry predator, Lil' Easy's hooded, bloodshot eyes took in every inch of Charli's six-foot frame, fixing her with a lustful gaze. Without breaking it, he motioned for Flash to send her over to him.

"Lil' Easy wants you all to hisself tonight," Flash informed her.

"As long as he knows the rules." She was not in the mood to be pawed over by a stoned rapper.

"Just give him his money's worth." He didn't understand why a woman would get off work and go fuck some no-good boyfriend for free, but got all prissy just because a paying client wanted to cop a feel.

Charli took a shallow breath and headed over to Lil' Easy's table. Though her hips swayed seductively, her eyes were a blank canvas, open to the interpretation of others.

The platinum-selling rapper sat back waiting for his show. Charli eased down the veil that covered her emotions, while focusing on the hot track. She turned, giving him the view they all wanted, letting her body interpret the rhythm and ride the beat. Her sensuous moves and exotic aura were a million times more captivating than any of the nearly naked, breast-enhanced hootchies who normally danced at strip clubs. She represented the difference between graphic and nearly X-rated, and erotic and enticing. From the outside she appeared to be a woman consumed by sexuality and caught up in its glorious rapture, while in truth, the only thing on Charli's mind were dollar signs.

She was abruptly snapped back into reality by all ten of

Lil' Easy's fingers as he groped her hips *and* her ass, clearly violating the "no hands" rule, while plotting the violation of quite a few others. "You do know club rules?" Charlie chastised.

He laughed arrogantly, fully displaying a mouthful of gold. "Rules are for other people."

"Club rules may be, but *my* rules are for everybody," she said, fixing him with a firm gaze.

He found Charli and her comment both interesting and intriguing. It wasn't often that a woman—especially a stripper!—denied him anything. "So, what are your rules?" he asked, clearly amused.

"First off," she replied, not missing a beat, "I'm not for sale."

"And second?" he challenged.

"If I were, it wouldn't be to you."

"Ten thousand dollars *cash* says that you'll meet me in the private suite." He stood up. "You've got five minutes." He never looked back as he picked up his drink and his blunt and left for the private room.

Charli stood dumbfounded. Ten thousand dollars! That was a lot of money to turn down, but it was also understood by all of the dancers that you entered the private suite at your own risk. She could feel the eyes of the other dancers as they waited to see if Miss High and Mighty was prepared to get down and dirty.

Chapter 9

The next morning Rowe didn't look any better after ten full hours of sleep, if anything he appeared even more drained and lethargic than the day before. With mounting concern, Reese spoon-fed him a little chicken broth after he flatly refused to eat his favorite cereal, Trix, which really worried her. Rowe loved Trix! She was considering calling Chris, when the phone rang.

"Madam, the phone's for you," Gretchen said, quietly. She, too, was alarmed by his listlessness. Even when he'd had the flu last year, he was the same mischievous little boy, trying to hold his cough medicine in his mouth long enough to spit it out unnoticed. The little boy lying in the bed this morning was only a shell of himself.

"Hello?" Reese answered anxiously.

"Hi, Reese. It's Dr. Young."

Reese was immediately seized by panic. Under normal circumstances Dr. Young wouldn't be the one calling with test results. His nurse, Wendy, always took care of that. Plus, she didn't like the tone of his voice. It had that "I'm bracing myself to deliver bad news" sound. "Hi, Dr. Young."

"How's Rowe this morning?"

"He seems to be about the same, if not worse," Reese answered, as she fought back tears. It broke her heart to see him lying there so lifeless.

"That's what I thought," Dr. Young said under his breath.

"What's wrong with my baby?" Reese demanded.

"I need you to meet me at Cedars-Sinai. We need to get Rowe checked in and figure this all out."

"What's going on?" she demanded.

"Rowe's blood work was not what I expected, and I'd like to admit him right away. I'll explain it all when you get to Cedars-Sinai."

In slow motion, buried under a feeling of dread, Reese hung up the phone, took a deep breath, and ordered Gretchen to prepare Rowe for a trip to the hospital. The color drained from Gretchen's face, but she said nothing and quickly left to pack a bag and get Rowe ready to leave right away.

Reese picked up the phone and called Chris.

"Hi, what's up?" he asked.

Reese could tell that he was probably in the middle of working out, which he did daily during basketball season. One thing she had to credit him for, as a father, no matter what he was doing, when she or Rowe called, unless he was in the middle of a game-winning slam-dunk, he always picked up the phone. He had always been there for his son emotionally, as well as financially.

"It's about Rowe," she answered quietly.

"Is everything okay?" Urgency replaced distraction in his voice.

"I'm not sure. We're on the way to Cedars-Sinai now to meet Dr. Young."

"Cedars? Dr. Young? What the hell is going on?"

Reese explained the events of the last two days and promised to call him as soon as she knew more.

An hour later, a listless Rowe was checked into Cedars-Sinai, and his anxious mother was seated across the desk from a very worried-looking Dr. Young.

"I'd hoped that Rowe had a mild infection or some type of virus, but I'm sorry to have to tell you that the test results reveal a much more serious problem."

Reese prepared herself for the body blow that she saw coming. "What's wrong with my son?" she asked, even though a part of her did not want to hear the answer.

"I'm afraid that Rowe has an advanced and severe form of acute lymphoblastic leukemia."

Instead of the body blow she'd braced for, Dr. Young's words were like deep stab wounds right to her heart. She suddenly felt clammy all over, and her breath came in short rapid spurts, propelling Dr. Young to her side. Hugging her, he said in a soothing voice, "We are going to do everything that we can for Rowe, know that."

"What does that mean? Is it curable? Is he going to die?" Just saying those words released a dam of tears.

Dr. Young signaled for a nurse to bring Reese a glass of water and held her hand until she'd calmed down enough to comprehend the challenge they faced. "Though Rowe's leukemia is very aggressive, it can be cured, with an equally aggressive medical regimen."

"What do we have to do?" Some of the fight in Reese was coming back. She was prepared to do whatever was necessary to save her child.

"I'm recommending a course of chemotherapy, followed by a bone marrow transplant."

"Why both?"

"Frankly, given the severity of his case, I don't expect the chemo to cure it, though it could slow it down."

"Just tell me what I need to do."

"I'll need you and Rowe's father to be screened as donor matches, in preparation for the bone marrow transplant."

"Why does he have to be screened? I'll be the donor. I'll do anything for my son."

"I know that, Reese, but donor matching is a very complicated process. Typically, siblings offer the best chance of a good match, with parents offering secondary potential. Since Rowe has no siblings—does he?" Dr. Young verified.

"No." Reese shook her head.

"Then you and your ex-husband—whom I assume is Rowe's father?" he paused for affirmation.

Reese hesitated slightly before saying, "Yes, of course."

"Well, you two offer the next best options. You see, matches are determined based upon what we call human leukocyte antigen typing, or HLA. These HLA markers are found on most cells in your body. Your immune system uses them to recognize which cells belong and which ones do not, which is why it is critical that Rowe has the best match to avoid rejection. Then they will be able to boost his immune system and fight off the leukemia cells."

"Since I'm his mother, why can't he just use my marrow for the transplant?" she pleaded, not really comprehending the medical nuances.

"It's possible that he can, but I have to warn you that just because you are his mother, that doesn't mean that you'll have enough marker matches to be a suitable donor, which is why we need to test Chris as well."

"How much time do we have?"

"Not a lot," Dr. Young answered honestly. Concern was etched across his face. "If Rowe's condition worsens, it could be hard to reverse it."

"I understand."

"I'll get a round of chemo ordered up right away and you make arrangements to set up the tissue and DNA typing for you and Chris."

Reese nodded her head in resignation. As much as she loved her son, there was one request from Dr. Young, which could save Rowe's life that she'd rather not fulfill. Screening Chris as a donor match could be the kiss of death for her, since there was a good possibility that he *wasn't* Rowe's father.

Chapter 10

The publicity campaign leading up to the Academy Awards was nonstop and grueling. Not only was there a grinding schedule of interviews and appearances scheduled by the studio, but Brandon also had Lydia and her agency on overdrive. He intended for Gillian to bring home that little golden statute at whatever cost.

Meanwhile Gillian was discovering that those costs could be quite substantial. The heightened press meant that her every move and utterance was documented, dissected by the media and immediately transmitted around the globe with the help of weeklies, dailies, entertainment and cable talk shows, and, of course, the ever-important Internet.

This lesson was learned the hard way the day she was headed down Rodeo Drive with an array of shopping bags from Michael Kors, Narciso Rodriguez, Anna Sui, and Nanette Lepore, when her cell phone rang. While trying to retrieve it from her purse and manage the smorgasbord of designer goodies at the same time, she stumbled and nearly took a nasty fall. If not for a particularly handsome Italian, she and her shopping bags would have been spread out along the ritzy boulevard. Instead Michael, Narciso, Anna, and Nanette all tumbled to the sidewalk, just as Mr. Olive Complexion reached for Gillian's arm, catching her just before her fall. As he did, she looked into the deepest set of blue eyes she'd ever seen. The color seemed Photoshopped.

"Are you okay?" he asked. His sexy Italian accent was like a warm sponge bath the way it gently caressed her.

"I'm, I'm fine," she stammered. "Thank you."

They both stooped to pick up the wayward bags, rising at the same time and coming eye-to-eye, nearly nose-to-nose.

"Excuse me," Gillian said, stumbling in her haste to stand up and escape.

"I'd excuse you for anything," Mr. Blue Eyes said, never batting one of them.

For seconds that felt like an eternity, Gillian was transfixed by him.

"Thank you, Mr. . . . , I didn't catch your name."

"I'm Sebastian." He flashed that damned smile again. "And you are?"

"Gillian," she said. She suddenly remembered who she was, and where she was. "Thank you, again," she said, taking the bags from his hand. She turned abruptly and quickly dashed into the garage where her car was parked.

By the time Gillian had a quick bite to eat at the Ivy, and stopped off at Barney's on Wilshire Boulevard, the media's scintillating take on her shopping mishap had been captured digitally, washed thoroughly, spun out of control, then hung up to dry. She could feel the cool breeze when she joined Brandon in his study, where they had their predinner cocktail each evening.

"What the fuck is this?" he demanded. His well-cultivated veneer of sophistication was missing in action.

Gillian caught the paper that he tossed at her. Still ignorant, she asked, "What is it?" She was really taken aback by his anger. Since they met and married, Brandon had never even so much as raised his voice to her, let alone cursed. He'd always been in total control, keeping his darker side well under wraps.

"You tell me," he answered with a sneer.

Gillian focused on the wrinkled pages long enough to see a photograph of herself gazing into Sebastian's azure blue eyes. Anyone looking at the photo would understand on a visceral level that the two people pictured were very attracted to each other. Pictures didn't lie, so Gillian attempted to. "This was nothing," she said, "I was walking down Rodeo, tripped, and this guy—I don't even know his name—was nice enough to stop and help me."

Not very deep underneath his expensive, custom-tailored suit, Brandon was a street thug who was raised to live and die by his instincts, and right now they told him there was a serious problem at hand. "Don't bullshit me, Gillian," he snapped.

She'd never heard this nasty tone from her husband before, nor had she ever seen him look so menacing. Though, if she were completely honest with herself, she'd have to admit knowing that he was capable of it. Wasn't the evidence proving that he'd laundered money from drug dealers enough? Gillian had chosen to keep her head buried in the sand and well away from the compelling evidence that her husband was a drug-dealing thug who'd bought his way into the inner sanctums of Hollywood with bloodstained money. But she'd made her deal with the devil, and now she had too much at stake to undo it, and renegotiating was not an option.

"I'm not bullshitting you! I slipped. He caught me. End of story," she insisted.

"Not according to Gossip247.com." He jabbed at the print.

The headline read, "Oscar Nominee, Gillian Tillman-Russell, Finds Love on a Two-Way Street." The next few sentences told the reader how she and the "Italian Stallion" bumped into each other and, after lustfully staring into each other's eyes, had a private conversation then both left via an enclosed parking garage. Gillian couldn't believe what she was reading! They made it sound as if they fucked in the street, then left together for an encore. "I don't care what this says," Gillian spat back, "it is not what happened. You of all people should know what the press is capable of!"

"I'm not married to the press. I'm married to you, and I don't *ever* want to be humiliated like this again." He turned and stormed out of the room, slamming the door behind him. Gillian was left shaken and stirred, as well of in need of a very strong cocktail.

Before she could regain her composure, in walked Imelda. "What is going on?" she asked, covered in concern, along with a deep-hydration mask. Early evening was her beauty time, when she'd have aestheticians, manicurists, and a masseuse come to the house to help get her back into fighting shape before their big night.

"Nothing for you to be concerned about," Gillian said.

Not to be put off, Imelda took the paper from Gillian's hand, read it, and began pacing. "Gillian, what were you thinking? You're going to ruin everything!" By everything, she meant the nice, comfy and cozy life she enjoyed at her son-in-law's considerable expense.

"Nothing happened! I almost tripped. He caught me. My bags spilled. We both picked them up. End of story!" This refrain was already getting exhausting.

"I'm sure that's what you told Brandon," Imelda whispered. "But it's *me* you're talking to now." She gave her daughter a knowing look.

Gillian sighed and shook her head in disbelief.

Imelda continued, "I could have written the book on sexual attraction, and it's clear to me that something was going on here, even if it also ended here. Remember, Brandon is no fool, so I'd suggest that you stay well away from the opposite sex, unless of course the man's richer and more powerful than your husband." Imelda was the ultimate gold digger, never shy about sourcing a richer vein.

Before Gillian could respond, Imelda went on. "We've got to do damage control with the press. If you don't win that Oscar, Brandon's going to be very disappointed."

What about me, Gillian thought, but said aloud, "Maybe I should call Lydia."

"That hack? Please!" Imelda huffed. "If she weren't so inept this wouldn't have happened. Any decent publicist controls the press. If she had any relationships, she would have had a head's up on this and been able to negotiate her way out of it, and we wouldn't be in this position."

Just then the butler walked in. "Mrs. Russell, you have a phone call. A Miss Lydia."

Imelda snatched the phone from him, put one hand on her hip and barked, "Lydia? You're fired!" She'd been waiting to say that ever since Lydia kept her off the red carpet at Gillian's party. Firing her was the only way to make sure that it never happened again, especially on what could be the most important night of her life: the Academy Awards.

Chapter 11

Though Charli was ten thousand dollars richer, after an hour in the private suite with Lil' Sleazy, she felt degraded, dirty, and cheaper than a two-dollar whore. He, though, was on top of the world! Homeboy was laid back on a chaise with his pants still gathered around his ashy ankles, sucking on a blunt; he was clearly pleased with his purchase. A used condom lay strewn on the floor.

"Yo, shawty, yo shit is tight!" he drawled.

Surely he didn't expect a thank you for that crass compliment, so Charli ignored him and continued to dress, barely managing not to throw up the fast food she'd inhaled before darkening these doors. The image of him grunting above her certainly was bad enough, but the memory of actually kissing his acidic, gold-laden mouth totally turned her stomach. As it rumbled irritably, she quickly grabbed her cover. She was so anxious to leave the gutter that she had forgotten the hard-earned money that had lured her there.

Lil' Sleazy tossed it into the air making it rain hundred

dollar bills. He laughed as Charli hurriedly bent over to pick them up from the floor. She'd never felt as low in her entire life, like a mongrel dog pawing through trash for bits of left-over scrap. After gathering the crumbled bills, she scampered out the door, his derisive laughter following right behind her. He obviously took some kind of sick twisted pleasure in her humiliation. He'd heard from her jealous coworkers that she was too good to do anything but let paying clients look, but he'd always known that for the right amount of money, any woman was nothing but a ho.

Charli raced out of the club after grabbing her bag, barely restraining a stream of tears as the rapper's rancid smell oozed like lava from her pores. When the door of her Porsche was closed tight and securely locked, the floodgates opened, releasing a torrent of tears. She cried uncontrollably, mourning her life, as it was, as well as the lingering emptiness that had trailed her like a darkened cloud, and for the sense of loss that she'd endured her entire life, even after escaping Miner, Missouri, for the big city.

A car full of rowdy men pulled up to the club already drunk and looking for raunchy adventure. Charli turned on the engine and was ready to gun it out of the driveway before her phone rang. Pulling it from her bag, the LCD told her that the call was from Miner. Not good. As far as she was concerned, no good news ever came from there.

"Hello?"

"Charli?" The voice was a low-frequency beacon reaching out to her from the distant past. "This is your aunt Vioni."

Charli hadn't heard from her mother's sister in over five

years, so she was startled by the call. "Hi, Auntie, how are you?" she asked, subconsciously pulling together the slight fabric that clung to her breasts. If Vioni or her mother had any idea what she had just been doing they would both die from toxic shock.

"I'm fine, honey, but your mom is not so good."

"What's wrong with mom?"

"She's had a stroke. You'd better get home quick."

Charli's throat was suddenly constricted, causing her to grasp for every breath. The tsunami of tears from earlier had left her emotionally drained, but this newsbreak was taking her to a new low that she never knew existed. The feeling of despair and tenuousness that had reverberated like a soundtrack throughout her life was now amplified tenfold. Though she and her mother had had their differences, she was the only person that Charli had ever felt any connection to; without her there would be nothing.

Four hours later she was on an Air Tran flight from Hartsfield-Jackson International Airport, headed to St. Louis, stoically ignoring the slouch next to her who seemed determined to engage her in solicitous conversation but couldn't keep his eyes from wandering south of her face. After landing she took the BART shuttle service another two and a half hours into the heartland of America, riding by fields of corn and soybeans. The two women who shared the large van with her prattled on about the culinary advantages of Velveeta cheese and the new La-Z-Boy recliner one of their husbands had just put on layaway. Charli couldn't wait to get out of the boondocks, even though she hadn't yet stepped foot on its soil.

She remembered feeling the same way after graduating from high school with the knowledge that if she didn't escape immediately, in a matter of a few years, she, too, would become a walking, talking zombie with a tiny house full of dull kids and a boring husband who would become fatter and more boring as time went on. She only had to look at her mother for confirmation of these dismal realities.

Teresa was the wife of a small-town preacher, who never had a bad thing to say about anyone, not even her tyrannical, now deceased, husband. It was only when Charli showed relief rather than grief at his funeral that Teresa had any clue that there had been any problem in her predictably Stepford household. When she pressed her daughter for an explanation she heard the sad and pitiful story of a frightened little girl who was too terrified to disappoint or confront the man who had snuck into her room in the middle of the night to play hide-and-seek for years, yet was revered by everyone in the community. The only thing that Teresa said was that they should pray for his soul. Charli would much rather have spit on his grave instead.

"Where is she?" Charli demanded after storming into the hospital where her aunt sat waiting.

"She's down the hall, but I have to warn you that it doesn't look good. The doctors don't expect for her to hang on much longer."

A nugget-sized knot formed in Charli's throat. She'd honestly never considered the day when her mother wouldn't be there, no matter the distance between them. "Is she conscious?"

"She's in and out. When she is conscious she keeps asking for you, so I'm glad you made it here in time."

She took Charli's hand and led her to an intensive care room at the end of the hall. When they walked in Charli's breath caught in her throat at the sight of her mother. She looked like a demented experiment in a mad scientist's lab. Her sunken face was twisted and her mouth left partially open. A stream of drool escaped one side and her eyes seemed to be staring at something only she could see.

"Mom? Mom, can you hear me?" Charli pleaded when she finally moved past the shock of seeing this grotesque parody of her mother. For the second time in eight hours tears streamed down her face.

Slowly, Teresa's glassy eyes struggled to focus on the here and now, rather than that which lay somewhere beyond the physical world.

"Mom, it's me, Charli," she pleaded.

Teresa's eyes flickered in recognition. "A, Aaarrli . . ." The words barely escaped her twisted mouth, which now refused to form hard consonants.

"I'm here, Mom. Everything's going to be okay."

She tried to shake her head from side to side, denying Charli's words.

"It will," Charli insisted, more to herself than to her mother. Looking at the remnants of the woman she'd always loved, but not understood, she knew that nothing would ever be okay again.

"Lisssten," her mother said, then fell quiet, as if gathering her waning strength to continue. Her breath was labored, each one harder than the one that came before it.

"Mom, you need to rest. I'll be right here."

Teresa grabbed Charli's wrist with a surprising amount of her remaining strength. "Aarli . . . must know . . ."

"Rest, Mom," Charli insisted. She was alarmed by the tormented distress that had fallen on her mother's contorted face.

"Ou ust owe . . . ur . . . adopted . . ."

Charli's world came to a complete stop, as she struggled to comprehend that last word which was spoken. She was dumbstruck. No words could convey the overwhelming shock she felt, while at the same time there was a teasing sense of relief. An explanation was now provided for the strange feelings of detachment that had always plagued her odd relationship with her mother, and perhaps a feeble explanation for how her father could have done the vile things to her that he had.

She sank into the chair at her mother's bedside. Thoughts, both old and new, swirled around her. Charli was confused by unhinged reality, and was desperate to reconcile the incomplete puzzle of her life.

Teresa's admission, the unburdening of a decades-old secret, seemed to suck the remaining air from her deflating soul. "Ore . . . ," she tried to say. She was now gasping for breath, as her eyes fluttered in their weak and vain attempt to stay open and focused.

"Ore?"

In a valiant effort she said, "More . . ."

"What is it?" Charli asked, though she wasn't sure she really wanted to know. What more could there possibly be? Hadn't she suffered enough?

The last of Teresa's deathbed confession was but a gasp of breath.

Whatever the last secret was, she took it with her all the way to the grave.

Chapter 12

"If there is *anything* at all that Brandon and I can do to help, please don't hesitate to call. You know we'll be here for you," Gillian said.

"I know." Of that fact, Reese was sure. Following the car accident Gillian took Reese into her home, saw to her every need, hired a private nurse who traveled with them from L.A. to New York, where she was living at the time, and then stayed for a month to make sure that Reese was okay. Even though Reese had always been closer to Paulette, and Gillian to Lauren, there was still a strong bond that made a crisis for one a crisis for all.

Even through the thorniness of their petty jealousies their relationships survived. They were friends and sometimes fauxs but they always came together when it mattered.

"It's not as if you don't have your own problems, with this Oscar business and especially with the press introducing the world to your new boyfriend," Reese noted. Even after spending only two hours at Gillian's she could feel the tension throughout the house. Who knew that being a famous actress could be stressful?

"New boyfriend? What are you talking about?" Gillian asked.

"You know, the Italian Stallion guy." Hanging out at the hospital with Rowe gave her plenty of time to catch up on the scandal sheets and entertainment magazines. She'd probably read them all. "Hey, I understand the need to sometimes get a little extra. At least, I used to. Lately, I haven't had *any*, so I can't even imagine extra."

"Reese, don't believe everything you read. I don't know that guy. I had never met him before and haven't seen him since."

"You could have gotten his number for me," Reese teased. It felt good to at least for a few minutes think of something other than her and Rowe's dire situation.

"Trust me, getting his number was the last thing on my mind."

"How are things with you and Brandon?" Reese sensed a tension between them that she'd never felt before.

"Okay, I guess. You know this whole Oscar business is taxing, especially with my mom being here, and of course the tabloids aren't helping very much at all. But, hey, my problems are minuscule compared to what you're facing."

"I just had my bone marrow donor testing yesterday. I'm just praying there are enough markers so that I can be Rowe's donor."

"If not, you've got Chris as a backup." When Reese

didn't respond, Gillian gave her "the look" and asked, "He has been tested, right?"

"Not yet," she answered sheepishly.

"What do you mean not yet? He's Rowe's father! You have to test him. What could you be thinking?"

"What if he's not Rowe's father?" Reese asked quietly, battling back an army of fear and regret. She'd never admitted the possibility that Rowe wasn't Chris's son to anyone, not even herself. Instead, she'd lived blissfully in denial; choosing to believe the fairy tale that her husband had indeed fathered her child.

Gillian was shocked. "Are you telling me that Rowe is not Chris's father?"

"I'm saying there's a possibility that he isn't." She deeply regretted the stupid onetime liaison after a night of too many glasses of Champagne. Even in her inebriated state, she had remembered to demand a condom, but, as luck would have it, the damn thing broke. A month later she learned that she was pregnant and decided not to even entertain the idea that it might not be Chris's baby.

"Reese, he's gotta be tested!"

"What if he finds out that Rowe isn't his son? Those hefty monthly checks would stop quicker than he could speed dial his lawyer."

"Listen to me, Reese," Gillian implored, holding Reese by both shoulders, eye to eye. "You have got to put your son's life ahead of money. It's that simple." For someone who grew up with a mother who sometimes didn't, the choice was crystal clear to Gillian.

Tears burned the inside of Reese's lids, finally flowing over and down her cheeks. "I know," she said, quietly. "I know. I'm just praying that I'm a match and that we won't even have to go down that road."

"But what if you're not?"

"I'll say a prayer and have Chris take the test."

"What have you told him so far?"

"I gave him the diagnosis but didn't tell him the complete severity of it. He knows that Rowe is scheduled for a round of chemo tomorrow, but he doesn't know that a bone marrow transplant is imminent, and hopefully, by the time he finds out, I can also tell him that I'm a match and will be the donor."

"I pray that you are right," Gillian said, holding Reese's hands in hers.

"So do I," Reese said, "so do I."

Chapter 13

"I'll see you later," Mildred said to her husband, who sat in the wood paneled library beside a roaring fire with his nose buried in the *Wall Street Journal*. "I'm going shopping."

He barely acknowledged her presence, simply nodding his head in response.

All the better, she thought, as she made her escape on a pair of snakeskin Jimmy Choos. The house could burn down around them, as long as he had a balloon of cognac, a cigar, and his stockbroker on speed dial, nothing else would matter. Theirs had long been more of a leveraged merger than a loving marriage, but since their Lauren left the country and Paulette died, their distant union was more fragile than ever. Their only son, Gregory, had run out of the closet at age twenty-one, escaping Mildred's clutches, and never looked back. He hadn't been home from Europe in over ten years, not even for his grandmother's or Paulette's funerals.

Mildred soldiered on, convinced that her wayward

children would eventually see the light. As for her husband, their arrangement suited her just fine. She climbed into the lush Mercedes CL600 and tooled down their long, winding, and perfectly manicured driveway, past the staff of gardeners who tended the grounds even in the middle of winter. It would be a shame to have an errant leaf linger too long anywhere on the fifteen acres of prime Westchester real estate that the Baines family called home.

Bach oozed out of the custom speakers as she eased down the Cross Country Parkway. Forty minutes later she was pulling up to the valet at the Hudson on Fifty-eighth Street and Ninth Avenue. She climbed out looking more svelte than sixty years would suggest. Mildred was the ultimate cougar, known to turn the heads of men half her age. A lifetime of private trainers, weekly facials, and an unlimited budget could do that for a woman. Pleased with the appreciative glance from the valet, she smiled, though her large Dolce & Gabbana sunglasses hid the twinkle in her eyes.

Heading up the neon lit escalator and into the dark, cavernous lobby, she turned left and headed straight for the private elevators. Once on the twentieth floor, she took a right toward the end of the hallway, going to the corner suite. She felt a tingling sensation at the mere thought of what lay inside of it.

Three short raps on the door, and it magically opened. Her host remained behind it, careful not to be seen by anyone who might happen to be passing by at the same time as their rendezvous. Mildred strolled into the invitingly appointed suite and could smell the essence of him even before seeing or feeling his presence. Before she removed her glasses or sat her Birkin bag down, he pulled her into a passionately rough embrace.

"I guess that means you've missed me?" she said when they finally pulled apart.

"No, *this* means I've missed you," he answered, taking her hand and placing it over the ten inches of muscle that had been known to bring Mildred to her knees.

"Mmmmmmm," she moaned in anticipation of what was to come, literally. "I think I need to check on my friend."

She dropped her cashmere car coat onto the sofa before beginning to slowly unbutton her silk blouse. As she revealed more and more of her cleavage, her thickly lashed eyes never left his. He was still the most deliciously handsome man she'd ever seen.

Mildred was not a serial adulteress; in fact, this was her first and only affair. She'd had many opportunities, but sex had never been very high on her list of needs. Two sluts— Paulette and her mother—in the family were certainly enough. But there was something about this man—no matter how wicked their relationship was—that reminded her that she was a woman in a way that her husband never had. Having always gotten what she wanted her entire life, she saw no reason to deny herself now.

Mildred let her blouse slide to the floor. After cupping her lace-encased breasts, her hands continued southward, pushing aside her Herve Leger skirt, before shimmying out of it. She stepped toward him wearing only cream-colored French lingerie and sexy black pumps. Unlike the coquettish and immature girls that he probably bedded regularly, she was a woman who was in full command of her powers.

Mildred walked toward him slowly, kissed him deeply, and then slid to the floor, where the real show began. She opened his robe to discover that he was already completely naked beneath it, giving her complete access. She took him in her hands and proceeded to rub his hot flesh all over her face, deeply inhaling his strong masculine scent. Starting underneath, she lovingly bathed his length, and then warmed his balls in her mouth, while her tongue teased and her teeth lightly grazed. Slurping and sucking followed as she consumed him, desperately wanting to swallow every inch. He moaned and grabbed fists full of her hair, desperate to bury himself deep down her throat.

When she felt the throbbing and pulsating she stood up and kissed him deeply, wanting to make sure that he tasted himself, just as she had. He abruptly pushed her away, turned her around, and bent her over the sofa, thrusting himself into her with deep, urgent strokes. There was nothing loving about the way he took her, nor was there anything loving about how she gave it back; for both, it was sheer unadulterated selfish passion that drove them, all the way to orgasm.

Later, after they'd finally made their way into bed, she sighed. "You were absolutely fabulous."

He smiled to himself remembering what a selfish lover he'd been with most of his other conquests, but only because he didn't have to do anything to please them, just being there was generally enough. But Mildred was another story all together. She was not the kind of woman who'd settle for anything but the best, and that's what he gave her.

"Yes, I was," he laughed. "But so were you."

She turned to face him. "Now that the pleasantries are over with, I'll get to the point." She playfully caressed him. It was time for round two.

"Oh, is 'pleasantry' the new Park Avenue euphemism for sex?" he teased.

"For us it is, particularly given our secret history."

"In that case, may we have many pleasant returns."

He grabbed her and kissed her hard, while he grew long and strong. When she was breathless with desire, he headed south. After ten minutes of skilled oral ministrations, it was clear that this was a trip he took often. The man had crazy skills.

When he finally crawled up to reclaim her in one deep stroke, she tossed her head back and moaned, "Ohhhhh, Max . . ." just before she climaxed for the third time.

Chapter 14

Now that Imelda had summarily dismissed Lydia as her daughter's publicist, and because Gillian still stubbornly refused to hire a private assistant, Imelda promoted herself to Gillian's de facto right hand, at least until Brandon could find a suitable replacement for Lydia. Though it wasn't in Imelda's DNA to cater to anyone, she kept her eye on the prize and played her role to the hilt.

Sailing into Gillian's boudoir, she carried a brand new notepad and a Mont Blanc pen poised for some serious work. Gillian was lying on a chaise in the resplendent room with a satin sleeping mask pulled down over her eyes.

"Mom, you really should knock," Gillian said, without moving. She knew exactly who it was without even bothering to pull the mask away. Brandon had never entered her private sanctuary uninvited, so this annoying habit her mother had of bursting into rooms in *her* house was really quite irritating. The estate was certainly large enough that

Imelda's presence need not be felt; however, she seemed to be omnipresent.

"I *am* your mother," Imelda reminded her, even though she may have been better served reminding herself.

"I realize that, but this *is* my private dressing room." It was actually a bit more than that. It was Gillian's retreat, where she went to be alone, away from Brandon and the staff. Since the Italian Stallion article, she'd been spending quite a bit more time here, while Brandon seemed to be sulking, yet hovering at the same time, making her feel like a captive, and him a warden.

"Whatever. We don't have time to squabble over this. We have a very busy day." Imelda flipped her notebook open. "At eleven, we meet with Daniel Schwarz at the studio to review new scripts. At one we have that photo shoot with *Vogue*. And at six we meet with your stylist and Christian Siriano to discuss your gown for the awards ceremony," she rattled off.

"Cancel them all," Gillian said and rolled over toward the opposite wall. Between the press, Brandon's pouting, and the seriousness of Rowe's illness and Reese's deception, combined with her mother descending on them like Patton's army, Gillian's nerves were frayed. That sense of foreboding was now ever-present.

"Are you sick, or are you crazy?" Imelda snarled. There was no way that she'd let this spoiled brat of hers keep her from meeting the all-powerful and very single Mr. Schwartz or *the* Christian Siriano. After all, she had her own Oscar gown to worry about, too.

"Probably both," she shot back. "I'm sick of you and Brandon acting like this is your award and career, and I'm probably crazy to be married to him and to put up with you." There she'd said it.

"You ungrateful . . ." Imelda was truly taken aback that her daughter was being so selfish and didn't appreciate everything that she had. She certainly didn't appreciate the nine months of torture or the residual stretch marks it took to bring her into the world. She could have gotten rid of her, but she didn't—though, truth be told, the only reason she didn't was because she needed to bring a baby home from the hospital to hold on to the piece of husband she had at the time. Thank God she'd met her second husband six months later and was able to run away with him to a far bet-ter life. And she'd even taken Gillian with her when she could have left her behind in that small hick town in North Carolina! Then she wouldn't be lying here whining about being nominated for an Oscar. The nerve! Clearly, if it weren't for her, Gillian wouldn't be living this fabulous fairy tale existence, so this little pity party really pissed her off. As far as Imelda was concerned, Gillian owed her very life, and everything in it, to her.

Gillian ripped the sleeping mask off of her face, expos-ing raw anger; after years of biting her tongue, she was fi-nally standing up to her mother. "Just so we're clear, I didn't *ask* to be born. Nor did I ask to be dragged around the world on all of your gold-digging expeditions, chasing one rich man after another."

"Though you sure seem to have been taking notes,"

Imelda sniped back, coolly looking around her at her daughter's extravagant boudoir, which was larger than the average New York City apartment.

"How dare you!" Gillian hissed. She'd never talked to her mother like that before, but these last weeks had truly stretched her patience and worn her nerves.

Imelda was the most passive-aggressive person Gillian had ever known. She would do something seemingly very nice for you, then squander all of the goodwill on the next fucked up thing she'd do to you, and get away with it by reminding you of her completely unsolicited prior generosity. Worse yet, she played up to Brandon like a dreamy-eyed teenage girl, though it wasn't his puppy-dog eyes that drew her in but rather the dollar signs she saw reflected in them. Sometimes Gillian felt as if her mother would sleep with him if it would ensure access to his wealth. She was forced to face the coldest and hardest truth of all: her mother was a cold-hearted opportunist who would throw anybody under the bus if it meant that her ride would be smoother, faster, and take her farther, even her own daughter.

"How dare *you*!" Imelda shot back.

Now they were toe-to-toe, and nose-to-nose, and Gillian was not backing down. After a few long and torturous seconds, Imelda realized that this was a battle she couldn't win, not here, not now, so she decided to hold her fire and retreat for the time being.

"Gillian, honey, I'm sorry, I didn't mean that," she finally said, lowering her head. "I am sorry for the mistakes that I've made in my life and, more importantly, for how they've affected you." She reached out to touch Gillian's forearm. "That's why I'm here now. I realize that I can't change the past, but I can try to make up for it by helping you take advantage of *your* opportunities." A swell of tears brimmed her eyes. She hoped that she hadn't overacted the part; the last thing she wanted to do was reapply eyeliner and mascara, and she certainly did not want to meet the head of a major film studio sporting red and swollen eyes.

Gillian was genuinely touched by her mother's words and sincerity, never realizing that her own acting ability hadn't materialized out of thin air. Like mother, like daughter . . .

"Would you accept my apology?" The doe-eyed look was priceless.

"Of course," Gillian said.

The two women embraced. Gillian clung to her mother, praying that this was truly a turning point for them. With Lauren being out of the country with Gideon so much, she didn't have anyone to really lean on, so she remained hopeful that she could count on her mother after all.

She realized that from afar fame and fortune seemed to make life so much easier, but the late Biggie Smalls had had a point when he said, "Mo' money, mo' problems."

Chapter 15

Her mother was hardly cold in her grave when Charli boarded the shuttle for the three-hour-long ride from Miner back to St. Louis's airport, hopefully for the very last time.

The days preceding the funeral were a surreal blur of activity as her aunt made arrangements for the service and burial, while evading Charli's questions about her mother, whom she now felt as if she never really knew. Aunt Vioni claimed that when her sister and brother-in-law moved to Miner, shortly after her birth, she had no reason to think that Charli wasn't their biological child, and that her sister had not once alluded to anything of the sort.

Going through her mother's personal effects, Charli searched for clues to her identity. The only thing she found, aside from childhood memorabilia, was her birth certificate, which listed Teresa and Henry Kemble as her parents. According to the document, she was born in Waynesboro, North Carolina, on June 7, 1976, and weighed five pounds

and ten ounces. Nothing surprising there. Maybe she'd mis-
heard or misunderstood her mother, after all her speech had
been severely hindered by the stroke, plus she was heavily
sedated and near death, so it was entirely possible that even
if she had said the word *adopted* that it was only a delu-
sional rant.

Charli hated the idea of being the clichéd adopted child,
who inevitably went searching for her real parents, but the
desire sprang up in her instantly. She wanted to know who
they were and why they gave her away. Sometimes she envisioned a loving young couple that was simply unable to take
care of her and had given her away as a sacrifice to ensure
that she had a better life. During her darker hours she wondered whether her natural father was also a pedophile, or
maybe something worse. She envisioned a young drug
addict/prostitute who'd given birth to her the way others
had a bowel movement, wiped herself clean, and then tossed
away the evidence. In either scenario she felt as discarded as
she had after being used by Lil' Easy.

Sitting in the window seat on the way back to Atlanta,
Charli fought back tears as she reflected on that awful night
before she left for Miner. After the call from her aunt, she'd
only been focused on getting to her mother's bedside, then
on the shocking bedside confession, and later on the funeral,
so this was the first time that she'd been able to reflect on the
demeaning hour spent with Lil' Sleazy. It still made her
physically sick just to think about it. Right then she decided
that as soon as she got home and showered she would march
right into the club, pick up her things, and leave for good.

It didn't matter that she had no idea what she'd do for work, or that she had no marketable skills to speak of (unless proficiency at the booty shake counted), or that she had no family or friends for support. She did have a bank account that thankfully had enough money in it to last her for a while.

Later that evening she walked into the club sans the shoulder-length wig that she normally wore to work, and without the extra heavy hand of makeup, or the garish clothes. Flash barely recognized her.

"I'm done," was all she said to him.

"You haven't even started. In fact you can't be coming to work looking like that," he frowned.

"You don't understand, I quit."

"You what?!"

"You heard me, I quit!"

"You gotta be kidding with that big payday you got last week." He chuckled. Not many hos get ten thousand dollars an hour for the puss.

"Read my lips, moron. I'm done, finished, finito." She turned to leave, aware of the clique of girls who stood nearby whispering as they watched the sideshow begin.

He grabbed her arm and swung her back around. Flash wasn't letting her go that easy. She was suddenly a very lucrative meal ticket. Lil' Easy had tipped him a grand after their visit to the private suite, and then assured him that he would be a regular behind its dingy doors for as long as Charli was there, too. He had to talk some sense into her. "Don't be stupid. Just because your mother died, doesn't mean that you should throw all of this away," he said gesturing at the sleazy joint as though it were the Taj Mahal.

"Let go of me," she demanded.

"Charli, listen to me—" he said, tightening his grip.

Before he could finish his sentence, the palm of her right hand met the side of his face in a resounding smack. His eyes bulged in surprise. How dare a whore slap him! A blind rage consumed him, he pulled his fist back, ready to take a swing, when a man grabbed him from behind and said, "That's enough. Let the lady go."

Relief filled Charli, knowing that most of the patrons and certainly none of the girls were planning to intercede on her behalf; in fact, most were sitting back waiting for the real action to start. Who cared that a ho was about to get her ass whipped?

"Who the fuck are you?" Flash demanded of the stranger.

"Don't worry about it, just know that you're dead if you put your hand on the lady again. Got that?"

The stranger took Charli's hand and ushered her out of the club. When they reached her car, she turned to him, still shaking, and asked, "Who are you?"

"I'm Max. Maximillian Neuman, the third," he said.

"Thank you so much," she whimpered. "I don't know what I would have done if you hadn't been there." Tears left a wet trail down her cheeks at the thought of being beaten on top of all the other indignities that she'd suffered.

For the first time, Max looked at her closely. "What's your name?" he asked.

"Charli. Charli Kemble."

A puzzled expression settled on his handsome features. "Where are you from?"

Suddenly weary, Charli dug in her purse for her keys, ready to leave the place and the stranger. She had never been comfortable answering questions from strangers. "Why do you ask?" She pressed the button to open her car door.

He backed up a step, realizing that she was feeling threatened and he did not want to scare her away. "It's just that you bear an uncanny resemblance to someone I used to know." He closely studied her features, ignoring the hair cut and color, which had been dyed black, and taking off about ten pounds, along with the layers of makeup, which were still a bit on the heavy side, and there standing before him was none other than the spitting image of *the* Gillian Tillman-Russell.

Chapter 16

Reese hadn't prayed, really prayed, to God, since she was twelve and wanted a pink bicycle for Christmas. It hadn't worked then, but she had to give it another try now, so she got down on her knees and prayed hard that her bone marrow would be a good match for Rowe, so she wouldn't have to pry open the Pandora's box of his paternity.

She grabbed a bag of Rowe's favorite games and books that Gretchen had packed and headed toward the door. Before she got there, the phone rang, which she planned to ignore, until Gretchen, ever dutiful, came running after her. "Mrs. Nolan, it's Mr. Nolan. He wants to speak to you."

She would much rather have done without speaking to Chris just now, but realized that this was not the time to be ignoring him.

"Hi, Chris."

"How's Rowe?" You could hear the fear in his voice clear across the continent. He'd wanted to fly out to the coast days ago when Rowe was diagnosed, skipping a few games, but Reese convinced him that it would be better if he kept things normal, so as not to alarm Rowe, who knew the Knicks' schedule better than Chris did. She'd promised to keep him up to date on everything that was happening and to make sure that they spoke at least twice a day.

"He had his first round of chemo yesterday. He was about the same last night, but definitely seemed drained this morning. I'm on the way to the hospital now, so I'll know more later today."

"They do expect this to cure it though, right?"

"Everyone is optimistic," she hedged. "Gotta run, I'll call you later." She wanted to avoid any more of his questions at all costs. Hopefully, when she called him later, she could tell him about the severity of Rowe's condition, the need for a bone marrow transplant, and the fact that she would be the donor.

Thirty minutes later she was again sitting across the desk from Dr. Young.

"I know how much you wanted to be Rowe's donor, and I understand that mother's need to fix everything, but in this case you can't. There weren't enough markers to make you a good match. We have to have at least six and you only had three. I'm sorry, Reese."

Reese felt as if someone had pulled the rug out from under her. She had really counted on this working, and wondered why God was punishing her so, but she only had to recall some of her past stunts to summon an answer.

Misreading Reese's deflated look, Dr. Young said, "Don't worry, Chris may be a viable donor, and we also have the national bone marrow bank to draw from. By the way, when is Chris taking his DNA tissue typing?"

Reese took a deep breath. "Dr. Young, I'd much rather go through the national bank."

Dr. Young gave her a puzzled expression. "Why? You may not realize it, but that is a lengthy process with many other applicants also in line, and frankly, Rowe doesn't have that kind of time. You have got to get Chris to take the test, or you're risking your son's life," he said bluntly.

"What if he isn't a match either?"

"We'll cross that bridge when we get to it, but first things first. Get him tested today."

Reese resigned herself to what was in the best interest of Rowe, even if it meant losing her monthly support. Now she could curse herself for spending so much of her settlement, but between buying and furnishing the house, the two cars, and what was left of her investments after the market tanked, she had very little to live on.

She sucked it up; after all, there was a better than even chance that Chris was Rowe's father. It didn't help that he looked exactly like her, showing no obvious signs of Chris or the man behind door number two.

"I'll call him right away."

"Good," Dr. Young said. "You can use my phone." He got up to leave the room, affording her some privacy.

With reticence, Reese dialed Chris's cell.

He picked up on the first ring. "How is he doing?"

"He's going to need a bone marrow transplant." She

decided to just spit it out, there was no sugarcoating the reality anymore.

"A bone marrow transplant? That sounds serious. I thought the chemo was supposed to take care of this." Concern was now replaced by fear.

"Dr. Young just feels that both will be necessary to give Rowe the best chance at recovery."

"So, what now?"

"You need to take a test to see if your marrow might be a match. As his parents, we are the best possibilities, though it's possible that neither one of us will be a match." Reese explained all of the technical jargon that Dr. Young had explained to her.

"I'll be on the next flight out. Would you do me a favor and make a reservation for me at the Four Seasons? It's pretty close to Cedars, so at least I can spend time with him," his voice cracked.

"He'll be okay, Chris. In fact, if you want, you can have the testing done right there in New York. They can call in the results to Dr. Young."

"Are you crazy? You're telling me that my son has a serious illness and you think I'm gonna stay away from his bedside?"

"But what about your games? This could all take a while. You should maybe wait until we know more before you take time off from the Knicks."

"Fuck the Knicks. I'll call you when I get to the airport," he said, then slammed the phone down.

Reese had rarely heard Chris raise his voice or curse. It sent an ominous shiver down her spine.

Later, when she got home, Reese got back down on her knees and again prayed to God, hoping that this time he might really hear her.

Chapter 17

Larry King sat forward wearing his trade-mark suspenders and that goofy smile he saves for attractive female guests. "So, tell us, Gillian, how does it feel to go from an unknown model to a famous Academy Award–nominated actress—all within two years?"

Gillian smiled demurely as she considered how to answer the question. Interviews were a landmine of possible gaffes, and without Lydia, she found herself tiptoeing through them very gingerly. Even without a publicist on board, Gillian, Brandon, and Imelda had agreed that she needed to do the show, since being on Larry King was akin to being accepted as a permanent fixture in American's collective imagination.

"All of the attention can be a bit overwhelming," she said. "Though I'm not complaining. I love what I do and am deeply appreciative for the fans who enjoy my work." One thing she realized was that the public despised a whining, overindulged, and pampered celebrity.

In typical Larry King style, he quickly shifted gears. "Most of us don't know a lot about you, so tell the viewers about your life growing up. I hear it's been quite interesting." He leaned back in anticipation of her story. This was her first in-depth, hour-long interview, which was quite a coup for King, since the media and everyone else for that matter seemed totally fixated on the exotically beautiful girl who'd burst onto the scene, stealing hearts and scripts alike.

This was where it got really dicey. She longed for Lydia, who—despite her shortcomings—always did a masterful job of prepping her for interviews. She could kill her mother for firing her, and herself and Brandon for not putting their foot down and hiring her back. She took a deep breath and tried to remember the party line that she and Brandon had agreed would work best. "Though I was born in North Carolina, I really grew up around the world. My mom and I lived in Paris, London, and Spain, so we did quite a bit of traveling."

"I suppose that would account for that inexplicable accent of yours." He was clearly enamored of her.

She favored him and his millions of viewers with her most charming smile. "I suppose so."

"How did it happen that you and your mom lived in so many cities around the world?" he asked.

This was the touchy part. "My stepfather lived in Europe," she answered simply, failing to mention the exact number of stepfathers. Under her circumstances, given the title of the movie, *Gold Diggers*, and how she conveniently married the producer and financier, the last thing she wanted to do was to give the impression that she'd been raised and schooled by a world-class gold digger, even though she had.

She knew that her mother was backstage watching the feed and praying that her name, rank, and serial number would be given.

"So he moved the family around?" It was a question that subtly got to the crux of the matter that Gillian wanted so desperately to avoid.

She couldn't say yes, since each move did precipitate the end of one relationship and the beginning of a more lucrative one. "After they divorced, we left Paris." Her goal was to give out as little information as possible.

"And rather than come home to the States the two of you struck out across Europe? That was very brave. How old were you at the time?"

She chose to ignore the first part of the question. "I was around five, I believe, when we left Paris." Her acting skills were truly coming in handy. No one—except Oprah Winfrey, Barbara Walters, Dr. Phil, and Larry King—would have seen the unease with which she'd answered that question.

"Did you see your biological father much?" he asked innocently. His acting was almost as good as hers.

She could feel the trap that was being set for her, but didn't know how to avoid its nasty snare. "No," she answered simply.

"Did you ever see him?"

"No."

"Have you two been in touch since you've become famous?"

"My father is deceased."

"And your stepfather?"

Which one? She thought to herself, but said, "I don't keep in touch." It was a very shrewd answer. It neither confirmed nor denied that there was only one stepfather, rather than five.

Larry let it go, not wanting to venture into the *Jerry Springer* vein of gutter journalism. "Tell us about your glamorous mother, Baroness von Glich, and the influence that she has had on your life."

This was more familiar, if not less treacherous, territory. "My mom is an amazing woman," Gillian fake-smiled. She could feel the pressure of a swiftly inflating ego emanating from backstage. "Through her I've learned how to appreciate different cultures and to have a genuine love of life, no matter its trials and tribulations." A heartwarming smile blossomed across Gillian's face. Forget that award-winning tear that Denzel shed in *Glory*, this was truly another Oscar-worthy moment.

Backstage Imelda was near orgasm. Her name, along with her title, had been mentioned glowingly on one of the highest rated and most well-regarded talk shows in the whole world. And the way he said her name! *Baroness von Glich . . .* she could tell that he must be attracted to her. But he was married, not that such a technicality had ever stopped her in the past. Her third husband had been the husband of her then best friend that evening when her Robert Clergerie-clad toe trailed northward up his leg during an intimate dinner that they shared with her and husband number two.

When it came to love and/or money, it was all out war with Imelda.

Meanwhile, back in Atlanta, Max and Charli watched the same interview equally attentively. She was in a similar state of shock as when her mother gave her deathbed confession, but this was even deeper. Though she'd certainly heard of Gillian Tillman-Russell over the last two years, she wasn't a moviegoer and thought that the celebrity tabloids were stupid, so she never read them. And while she may have seen a picture or two in passing, with Gillian's chic haircut, expert styling, and makeup, the resemblance between the two had never occurred to her. She did recall one of the rappers in the club telling her that she looked like an actress, but this was after so many shots of Hennessey he couldn't even remember her name, let alone his own. Watching Gillian on screen convinced her of what Max had been telling her for the last twenty-four hours: Gillian Tillman-Russell was her twin sister! He'd shown her photo after photo, but she wasn't convinced of it until she actually *saw* her sister. Forget the mannerisms and the speech patterns, Charli could *feel* the connection, through TV cable and across the continent. There was no doubt in her mind that they were sisters at the least, and more likely identical twins!

Chapter 18

"The Oscar-nominated actress Gillian Tillman-Russell seems to be hiding a family secret," Shaun Robinson shared with her viewers during an on-air teaser. "Stay tuned for this *Access Hollywood* exclusive."

Gillian, who had been going over a script with the TV on low, nearly popped out of her seat. A family secret! What on earth were they talking about? She marched into the spa, where she found her mother facedown on the massage table with two masseuses working her over. One Adonis look-a-like worked her back over, while the other gave his full and undivided attention to her legs. They were both gorgeous. She insisted on only having men massage her, and they had to be handsome to boot.

"Mom, you need to come quick," Gillian said, bursting into the room.

"Honey, I'm busy right now," she answered, turning her head to one side.

"I don't care. After a commercial, *Access Hollywood* is running a piece about some family secret I'm hiding."

This got Imelda's attention. She lifted her head. "Family secret? What family secret?"

"That's what I need you to tell me."

"I have no idea what they're talking about."

"In that case, let's go find out." She grabbed her mother's robe and handed it to her. Imelda very reluctantly got up from the table and followed Gillian out of the room. A squadron of butterflies swarmed in the pit of her stomach. What family secret could they be referring to she wondered.

Shaun was just coming back from commercial break when they entered the room. "It appears as if the beautiful and talented Oscar-nominated actress, Gillian Tillman-Russell, seems to have written a family member out of the story of her life. Earlier this week during an interview with Larry King, when asked if she'd been in touch with her biological father since becoming famous, the actress replied that he was deceased." A clip of that portion of the interview ran. "Well, *Access Hollywood* has learned that this is *not* the case. Arthur Tillman is very much alive and desperately wants to meet the daughter that he hasn't seen since she was an infant."

The video cut to a photograph of a paunchy man wearing a red plaid shirt, standing in front of a doublewide trailer.

"Mr. Tillman, why would Gillian say that you were dead?" the onsite reporter asked.

"Cain't say as I know," he answered, before spitting out a wad of tobacco.

"When was the last time you saw your daughter?"

" 'Twas shawtly afta she's bone. Her momma just ran off wit her and dis lawyer fella one day. Hadn't seen 'em since. Had no idea where in the world dey was."

"Would you like to see your daughter?"

" 'Course I wud," he answered. Arthur turned to face the camera, earnestly. "Gillian, baby, if you's out there in TV land, nos I luv ya, and I wants ta see ya."

Gillian's knees buckled. Thankfully there was a sofa behind her. She sat there for almost a minute in a stupor. Not only was the father that she'd been told died when she was a baby alive and kicking, but he was apparently a country hick living in a trailer in the backwoods of North Carolina. "How could you?" were the only words that she could form. She turned to face her mother, who seemed to be planted in the same spot, unable to move.

For once Imelda was speechless. It never occurred to her that the media attention that she craved so much would be a double-edged sword, fully capable of exposing her deepest, darkest secrets. Having left the United States so long ago, her old existence felt remote, as though it had happened to someone else. She'd run a long way from the poor, unsophisticated life that she'd led back then, but here it was waiting for her just short of the finish line.

"Say something!" Gillian demanded. Though her mother hadn't said a word, the truth was for once written all over her face. Gillian had always known that her mother was selfish and opportunistic, but she would never have thought that she'd be capable of something so low as denying her the right to know her own father.

"I don't know what to say, honey. To me he *was* dead."

"But what about me?" Gillian shouted. "You've always only thought about yourself. I deserved to be able to make my own choice, not one that was more convenient for you in your quest for the next rich husband." By now tears were streaming down her face. Knowing her mother lied to her her entire life about something so crucial, and had not batted an eyelash over it, hurt Gillian to her core.

"I'm sorry," was all that Imelda could muster. There was simply no defense for what she'd done. She couldn't tell her daughter the truth. That she wanted to run as far away from Arthur Tillman, and all that he represented, as she could get. And the closer and closer she got to the promised land, the more that the thought of him didn't fit into it. How could she possibly explain to Gillian that the mere sight of him would have hurt not only her own but both their images? Aside from being sorry that this all came out, her most honest emotion was embarrassment. She was deeply ashamed that the whole world now knew that Baroness von Glich was once married to that tobacco chewing, beer-bellied illiterate.

Chapter 19

This Tillman family bombshell was manna straight from heaven for Lydia. After Imelda fired her as Gillian's publicist, the snakes at her PR agency followed suit and fired her, too. One minute she was one of the most envied publicists in the world, and the next she'd been summarily dismissed, and then blacklisted. All of this doom and gloom, because of that privileged bitch Gillian, her nasty mother, Imelda, and that gangster wannabe Brandon Russell. To make matters worse, not only did she lose her job, but her fiancé suddenly postponed their wedding date, indefinitely, confirming her subconscious belief that he was only marrying her to have access to hot parties and A-list events. Initially, she blamed Imelda solely for her rapid descent into nobodydom, but soon decided that the *real* culprits were Brandon and Gillian for not standing up to Mommy Dearest. After all her hard work, they'd simply tossed her out like last season's wardrobe.

After days of stewing in her own juices, her rash festered

like a boil; her therapist told her that she should channel her anger. That's when she came up with the brilliant idea to write a tell-all book about the Hollywood power couple that would focus on who killed Gillian's friend Paulette, the larger-in-death-than-in-life publicist.

Besides having observed enough of the intimate details about the couple—little things that were amazingly revealing—Lydia had been an investigative reporter before becoming a publicist. In fact, thanks to a little spying she'd already done, she felt sure that she could add some juicy tidbits to the now-dead investigation of who killed Paulette Dolliver. Even though neither Brandon nor Gillian had been serious suspects, Lydia had a plan to link them to the murder and was sure she would sell a million copies of her book as a result. Besides, she didn't care if the case was ever solved, writing her book was only a convenient and profitable way to get back at two people whom she'd mistakenly thought had been her friends. That was the stark irony, by protecting Gillian from her young-eating, predator of a mother she'd end up being the one devoured. As some smart writer once wrote: Revenge *was* best served cold.

Within two weeks she'd written a compelling book proposal, contacted an editor at Celebrity Publishing, and was now a pen stroke away from signing the book deal, which, by the way, came with a fairly hefty advance. She picked up a straw, leaned over, and snorted up a line of powder-fine coke, chasing it down with a glass of red wine. Then she made a toast to herself. "Here's to *Lights, Cameras, and Action! The Story of Fame, Fortune, and Fatality.*"

She loved the charge of energy that cocaine gave her. The wine helped to take the edge off of it, making sure that the ride was fast, but smooth. This lovely cocktail was far better for her mood than the mix of Prozac, Ativan, and Ritalin the doctor prescribed. Besides, she needed the extra energy to meet her deadline. Though it was a serious rush, she and the publisher had agreed that the book had to come out the week before the Oscars, which meant that she had six weeks to write it, and with the help of a private investigator hired by the company, she would get it done, come hell or high water.

She signed all three copies of the contract and got right down to work. The "confidential" police files that her investigator had obtained were a treasure trove of juicy details that made for some very interesting reading. According to the report there had never been a shortage of suspects. Lydia nearly salivated over the scintillating details, or maybe the drooling was the result of the cocaine's numbing effect.

At the top of the detective's list was Maximillian Neuman III. Here was a real snake charmer. He's just the sort of man most women became addicted to. Max was the father of Paulette's unborn child, yet was married to her first cousin, Lauren, whom she was jealous of. Desperate to keep news of his bastard child and the scandalous affair quiet to preserve the millions he'd married into, Max had motive to spare. He could have gotten rid of the mother and the child in one fell swoop. But, since he was in New York at the time the car was tampered with, it would have been necessary for him to hire someone to do it. The investigator had never found a link to this person, so Max, at least so far, seemed to lack opportunity.

Next up on the list was Chris Nolan, the NBA superstar, whose now ex-wife, Reese, was also along for the tragic ride. It appeared as though she and Paulette had plotted to obtain embarrassing photos of Chris with another man to black-mail him into a larger divorce settlement than was required under the prenup. Now there's a motive for you: Again, two birds, one stone. Though the detective was unable to find any evidence showing how Chris could have pulled this off when his team was playing the Hawks in Atlanta that night and there was no evidence of a hired gun.

As far as Lydia was concerned, the suspect du jour was *the* Brandon Russell. He had ample motive, based on rumors that Paulette knew about his money laundering, and more importantly, he had opportunity, since the car was parked in *his* covered garage and he knew it would be, since the shower had been planned for weeks. Plus, given Gillian's superstar-dom, having him be the guilty party would certainly sell more books.

Lydia took another hit of coke and wrote:

> *Even before marrying a mega-rich media mogul and be-coming an Oscar-nominated actress, Gillian Tillman-Russell was accustomed to lights, cameras, and a lot of action. The former runway model grew up gallivanting around the globe with her flamboyant mother and a series of increasingly wealthy stepfathers. After her acting career failed to launch, Gillian married the wealthy film producer Brandon Russell,*

who used his money, power, and connections to make her the hottest new actress to grace Tinseltown. Before their "I dos" were exchanged—along with the brilliant ten-carat diamond ring—and before the red carpets were walked, amid throngs of frenzied paparazzi, Gillian must have wondered whether her smooth-talking Svengali was also a money-laundering schemer as alleged by authorities.

Hip hop impresario Brandon Russell is a hustler's hustler. Born in the squalor of Mississippi's ghettos, he used street smarts to transform a wannabe rapper's raunchy single into an iconic multimillion-dollar record label, and since then has taken up residence amid the pristinely manicured lawns of Beverly Hills. Underneath Brandon's Brioni suits and carefully crafted demeanor, quietly lies a ruthless and cunning manipulator whose skeletons may outnumber the expensive designer garments in his expansive walk-in closet. What about Gillian? Is her fairy-tale marriage a deal with the devil that she might be unable to keep? Or is she just as apt a wizard herself?

Lydia loved it. She felt powerful; with a keystroke she now had the ability to strike back at her enemies—and, unfortunately for her, multiply their number.

Chapter 20

"Gillian, look who's here!" Brandon said, gesturing to a tall, attractive, brown-skinned woman, who walked into the office alongside him. "CoAnne's agreed to rejoin the team."

CoAnne Wilshire had been Gillian's publicist from the start, but she left the business last year to be a full-time stay-at-home mom. It didn't take long for her to discover that slaying dragons on a daily basis was much easier than chasing a manic toddler.

Gillian nearly ran to the door, hugging CoAnne tight. It had been a while since they'd seen each other. "I'm *so* glad you're back!" Gillian said, truly meaning it. She'd gotten a harsh lesson in PR over the last couple of weeks and truly missed CoAnne's sound judgment and strategy.

"We've got to get busy, honey," she said, taking a seat at the mahogany conference table in Brandon's office. "There's a lot of work to do. I leave you guys alone for a year and look what happens," she teased.

Her direct approach was definitely refreshing, since nowadays everyone went out of their way to suck up to Gillian. CoAnne reminded her of Paulette—not only were they both publicists, but each had a take-no-prisoner's personality. "Well, let's get started," she said.

"First and foremost, I don't want you talking to *anyone* outside of your immediate family without discussing it with me first."

"What about my father?"

"Especially your father. I realize that you probably want to reach out to him, but we've got to manage that very carefully. First and foremost, we have to put it out there that you had no idea he was alive, otherwise you look like a blatant liar. Not exactly upstanding Oscar material."

"So, do we admit to the world that my scheming mother lied to me?"

"That's up to you, my dear, though we could insinuate that even *she* believed he was dead, if you don't want to throw her all the way under the bus," which was exactly where she belonged, CoAnne thought, based on what she'd heard about the shrew. After hearing through the very busy PR grapevine what happened to Lydia, CoAnne insisted to Brandon that Imelda not be allowed to attend *any* PR meetings.

For the first time since the introductions Brandon spoke up. "Do you think it's wise to have Gillian have any contact with the man at all? He looks like a country bumpkin, not exactly a boost to her glamour image."

Gillian turned and glared at him. How dare he talk

about her father, when his upbringing wasn't exactly in a country club! Then she realized that that was the very reason he didn't want her in contact with Arthur, it might just be too close for comfort, akin to looking in the mirror.

"It's imperative that Gillian initiate contact with her father, otherwise she will come across as a stuck-up, heartless little bitch, who the public will turn on quicker than you can say *All About Eve*."

Both Gillian and Brandon nodded in agreement.

"But what we can do is set some preconditions. We can have him meet at an undisclosed location that we select and secure, and we can have him sign a confidentiality agreement. And if you like, I can meet with him first to determine if he might have a hidden agenda."

"That sounds like a good idea," Brandon said, again nodding his head.

"Good, now for more pressing matters." CoAnne leaned back and fixed Gillian with an unrelenting stare. "Is there *anything* potentially embarrassing that I should know about?" she asked. "And we can talk privately if you'd prefer."

"No, this is fine. I have nothing to hide," she said, though she shifted uncomfortably in her chair.

"Are you sure?" CoAnne raised an eyebrow. "I can only help if I know what I'm up against."

"I'm positive," Gillian answered adamantly. Where was CoAnne going with this? Gillian wondered. She'd certainly had enough surprises lately.

Suddenly, Brandon sat up in his chair, knitting his brow. First his perfect wife was spotted on the streets with some slick-looking Italian stud, and then a country bumpkin father shows up. Was there something *else* that he didn't know about? He fixed her with a prematurely accusatory look.

"Then, can you please explain this before I have to?" CoAnne tossed three photos across the table. "They just appeared on the Internet this morning."

Gillian picked up one and Brandon picked up the other two. Their mouths dropped open in sudden shock. Each photo contained graphic nude shots of Gillian. In one picture she cupped her breasts suggestively, while staring seductively into the camera's lens. In another shot she was laid back on a red velvet couch with her hands between her legs and her back arched, seemingly in the throes of an orgasm. The third one showed her standing naked facing a wall. Her behind was on full display as she looked back over her shoulder wearing a come-hither expression.

Gillian's eyes were glued to the lurid pictures of herself. Pictures that she *didn't* pose for. She shook her head in denial, confusion muddling her thoughts. She was too stunned for words of denial to form in her brain and then leave her lips.

"Goddamnit, Gillian," Brandon hissed, tossing the pictures onto the table as though they were toxic. "How the fuck could you do this?" he demanded. The only thing missing was the steam that should have been spewing from his ears. He was livid!

"B-but, th-th-that's not me," Gillian stammered, still confused as to how photos that looked exactly like her weren't. If she were a druggie, she might have convinced herself that maybe at some point she took the pictures and just didn't remember. But she wasn't. She was a moderate wine drinker and had always stayed away from drugs.

"Don't lie to me, Gillian. It looks just like you." Brandon was beyond pissed off; his blood was boiling. After all he'd done to make her a star, she had to go and pull some fucking Paris Hilton shit. Not only could this destroy their chances of winning the Oscar, and taint her career, but now he looked like a damned fool.

He'd always relished the jealous gazes of other men whenever he was with Gillian, but now they'd surely be laughing behind his back instead. The whole world was going to see his precious Gillian naked. He felt like such an idiot. All this time he thought he had a princess, but Gillian was turning out to be more of a porn star pauper.

Through her confusion Gillian could clearly see that her husband had already tried and convicted her. "Brandon, I did *not* take these pictures," she insisted. When he didn't answer she narrowed her eyes and challenged, "Are you calling me a liar?"

"If the fucking shoe fits," he snapped. "Oh, but I forgot you didn't have on any shoes, or clothes, or fucking underwear for that matter."

She'd had enough. Gillian stood up ready to confront him and let the chips fall where they may. "Don't you dare talk to me that way!" she spat.

Wanting to avoid the clash of the titans, CoAnne stood up to intervene. "You guys, this yelling isn't going to help anything, so let's all calm down." She fixed Gillian with a stern look, until she sat back down in her chair. Then she turned to Brandon. "You know, there is such a thing as Photoshop. It is entirely possible that Gillian's image was altered to fit someone else's body. Need I remind you, this *is* the digital age."

Still fuming, Brandon at least leaned back in his chair.

"How do we prove it?" Gillian asked.

"I know an expert in digital fraud that I can contact. I'll also see if we can determine who put the photos up, that could help, too. Meanwhile, I'll put out a statement, something to the effect of, 'Mrs. Tillman is very upset by the blatant misuse of her image and will seek full recourse from those involved.' If anyone contacts you directly, you refer them to me, and if you're forced to say anything, it should be 'I don't comment on impending legal matters.' And Brandon, you should get your legal team on this as well."

For the first time, Gillian fully understood the full specter of gloom that descended on her that sunny Mediterranean day on *Midas Touch* after she was nominated. Somehow she'd realized even then that all that glittered wasn't gold; even small golden statues could be tarnished.

Chapter 21

Reese stood solemnly on one side of Rowe's bed holding on to his increasingly fragile hand, while Chris, eyes bloodshot red, stood on the other, barely holding on himself. Though Reese had called to tell him of the events over the last week, nothing could have prepared him for the sight of their energetic, vibrant son in such a gaunt, color-less, and motionless state.

"Daddy, when can I go home?" Rowe pleaded. Though he didn't know the extent of his illness, he knew that being in the hospital was not a good thing.

"Soon, son, soon. Dr. Young just wants to make sure that you're ready for soccer when you leave," Chris answered, choking back the threat of tears.

Thankfully, Rowe had drifted back off to sleep before the stream of tears emerged.

The last time Chris had seen Rowe, three weeks ago when the Knicks were playing the Lakers, he'd gone to one of Rowe's soccer games, where he'd been even more impressive than usual since his dad was looking on. The kid lying here now bore no resemblance at all to the one he knew so well. His flesh and blood.

Chris's millions of dollars, throngs of fans, and stratospheric fame meant nothing compared to the agony of watching his only child drift away from him. He didn't even bother to wipe away the torrent of tears that streamed unchecked down his face, then gathered around the collar of his shirt, where they lingered before being absorbed into the fabric.

Though she wanted to ignore Chris's presence in Rowe's critical care room, particularly since the testy question of paternity loomed ahead, Reese couldn't help but feel his misery, hurt, anger, and, most pressing, his love. There was no doubt that Chris loved Rowe in that unconditional way that all great fathers did.

At that moment guilt—an emotion she'd never wasted time on—consumed her. She wanted to cross to the other side of the bed, reach out to Chris, and hold him, and then apologize for how she'd used him, and maybe even tell the truth, that he might not be Rowe's father at all. But she stayed transfixed, glued to the spot where she stood.

"Rowe, can you hear me?" Chris asked.

There was a barely perceptible move as Rowe's eyelids fluttered weakly.

"The sedative has kicked in. It helps with the nausea and vomiting from the chemo," Reese explained.

Just then Dr. Young walked in the door and joined Chris on his side of the bed.

"He's going to be okay, right?" Chris pleaded, as though it were strictly the doctor's choice.

"We're going to do everything we can." Dr. Young patted Chris's back comfortingly.

"I took my test as soon as I landed yesterday."

"I know. We just got the results."

Both Chris and Reese pulled away from their grief for the moment it took to reach out for hope.

"You're not a match, either, Chris. I'm sorry," Dr. Young said, reaching up to pat Chris's broad, muscular shoulder. They visibly slumped. Truth be told, he would have given bone marrow and anything else he had to save his son, including his millions and his fame.

Reese almost ceased to breathe. She had prayed that Chris would be a good bone marrow match for Rowe. Now she prayed that the question of paternity would not be raised.

"So, what do we do now?" she asked, desperately wanting to change the subject away from matching, which was tenuously close to the conversation that she truly dreaded, DNA.

"Why don't you both go have dinner since Rowe is asleep now. We'll watch over him and if there are any changes, of course, we'll call you. Meanwhile, I've already started the search through the national database."

"But how long does that take?" Chris asked.

"It could take a while," Dr. Young admitted.

"Do we have that much time?"

"Possibly not."

Chris collapsed into the chair behind him, lowering his face into his hands. The tears ran down his face like an angry river. Rowe was the love of his life, the son he'd always wanted. And now that—thanks to Paulette and Reese—he'd been dragged out of the closet, it was unlikely he'd ever have another son to carry on his name and bloodline. And even if he could, no child could *ever* replace Rowe. He loved his son more than life itself and would without question lay his own life down for that of his child's.

"Reese, can I see you for a moment?" Dr. Young asked.

"Sure." They left Chris immersed deep in his well of sorrow.

Once they reached a private office, Dr. Young sat Reese in a chair on one side and settled himself into one on the opposite side. "Is there something you want to tell me?" he asked. His trademark warmth was nowhere to be found.

"What are you talking about?" Reese asked, though in her gut, she knew precisely what the good doctor meant.

"Somehow, I don't think this will be a news flash to you, but Chris is not Rowe's father."

Reese leaned back in her chair. There was really nothing much to say. Her worst fears had been realized, though not fully since Chris still didn't know the truth. "I wasn't really sure."

"Why didn't you tell me this last week?" he demanded, snatching his ever-present glasses off of his face.

"I was hoping that I was wrong."

"When your son's life hangs in the balance, hope isn't enough."

"What would it have changed?" Reese asked sheepishly.

"To begin with, I would have started the national search immediately, rather than considering that one of two parents might come through."

"So what do we do now?"

"I suggest that you begin by doing something that may be a bit foreign to you, and that is put your child's interests ahead of your own."

His words stung Reese, deeply. But there was nothing that she could say to defend herself. Her actions were simply indefensible.

"Who you sleep with is your business and not mine, but when your selfishness jeopardizes my patient's life, guess what? It does become my business. That being said, what I need to know is who *is* Rowe's father?"

"Why is that important?" Reese asked sullenly.

"It's only important if you give a damn about your son's life. Your mystery man could hold the key to it."

She had never considered that possibility, and the thought terrified her in more ways than one.

Dr. Young replaced his glasses and contained his mounting anger, since it would do nothing to cure Rowe. "Reese, finding a donor in the national database is a long shot, based on the amount of time Rowe has. Unfortunately, his disease is very aggressive, so his biological father may be his best hope."

The mere thought of divulging Rowe's father's identity was paralyzing to Reese. Not only would it affect her monthly checks, but worse, it would ruin a few other lives in the process. She'd lost so much in the last few years, and hurt so many people with her actions, that the inevitable devastation that revealing Rowe's father would cause was more than she could take. But if she truly loved Rowe, she couldn't think about anyone else.

Dr. Young stood up. "I'll leave you to think about that."

Reese stopped him before he reached the door. "Are you going to tell Chris that he isn't Rowe's father?"

"I would much rather you do that. My interest is in the welfare of my patient, which means finding out if his real father is a match. And for Rowe's sake, I pray that he shows up, and more importantly that he can help save his son's life."

This time he left the room, closing the door behind him, leaving Reese alone with her rattling skeletons.

Chapter 22

"That's it, baby, touch her breasts. That's it, right there," Max coached. His commentary was the soundtrack to the rapid snapping of pictures of Charli making out with another woman. The blonde seemed to really be into it, while Charli was merely going through the motions. Not that she'd never been with another woman, it was just that she felt very uneasy, given the circumstances.

After Max convinced Charli that Gillian and Imelda were in fact her sister and mother, he stoked the simmering flames of resentment and anger at being the one left behind. He riled her up with half-baked stories of the two of them jet-setting around the world, living the high life amid glamour, wealth, and royalty. By the time he pieced together the story, based on what little he remembered from conversations with Lauren, and then enhanced, Imelda was Princess Grace and Gillian was Princess Stephanie. How dare they gallivant around the globe without a care in the world, while poor Charli was stuck in the boondocks fighting off a pedophile father and dealing with a distant, religious fanatic but well-meaning adoptive mother. Before it was all said and done, according to Max, it was both Imelda *and* Gillian's fault that she was a stripper.

Once Max got her that far, the final leap out of her clothes and onto the Internet was but a hop.

"They owe you for what they did to you," he goaded, never acknowledging that as an infant, Gillian couldn't have been cognizant or the least bit responsible for the fate of her sister. Nor did he allow for the fact that she probably still didn't know that Charli existed. "You have to get back by hitting them where it hurts," he coached.

"Maybe I should just call them," she ventured.

"So they can humiliate you more, like they did your father? They told the world that he was dead! They don't give a shit about you. The only thing they care about is Gillian's career and winning that Oscar."

"There's nothing that I can do," she'd replied, feeling the way she'd felt her entire life: small, weak, and unable to control the world around her. She couldn't fathom how she could possibly take on a big celebrity like her sister and a fancy socialite mother.

"Remember this, Gillian's success is built on her image." He paused for emphasis. "And *you* are her spitting image, which means that you can manipulate that image."

Charli turned and looked into the mirror, closely studying her features. On one hand, she saw that she looked just like Gillian, but she certainly wasn't as put together, as polished or as glamorous. It was as if Gillian was live, and she was merely Memorex.

Max read her mind. "The only difference between you and your sister is money and style. By that I mean all you need is a good stylist and aesthetician—"

"What's an aesthetician?"

"Someone who specializes in skin care," he explained.

"What's wrong with my skin?" she asked, pouting. Now that she knew that her twin sister was a glamorous movie star, she felt more self-conscious about herself than ever. Like Gillian, she'd never been a typical beauty with long flowing hair and a light complexion. Lacking in confidence she'd failed to discover her true beauty, which went far beyond the ordinary. Even seeing her identical features on Gillian didn't convince her that she could be that, too. It was confounding how two people who essentially had the exact same DNA could not look alike at all. She chalked that up to the difference between growing up in the sticks versus globe-trotting through Paris, London, and New York.

Max held her gently. "There is nothing wrong with your skin, but in order for you to photograph like Gillian you have to do the things that she does. That means weekly facials to get that glow, it means a high-end hair stylist to get the right color and cut, and it also means losing five to ten pounds. After that, you'll have Gillian and your mother both in the palm of your hand."

"I don't know," she said.

"Trust me," he'd said, before kissing her so passionately

that her knees nearly buckled. Charlie had never met a man as polished, sophisticated, and smart as Max, who in fact had her in the palm of *his* hand.

That was three weeks ago, and since then the first salvo of nude shots had gone out and blown up the blogosphere, TV, and cable shows. Everyone seemed to be talking about the salacious nude shots of the celebrated actress Gillian Tillman-Russell.

Charli didn't have any idea that her and Max's little prank would cause such uproar. Controlling the world media was very scary, but it also made her feel a sense of power for the first time in her life.

Now it was time to take it to the next level. Gillian's publicist had put out a press release stating that the pictures had been doctored and weren't her, though no one could find an expert willing to say that, because they *weren't* doctored, yet they weren't *her* either. Of course, no one had figured out that Gillian Russell had an identical twin sister. Sometimes the answer to the puzzle is too simple.

"Let's get one more shot of you and Mitzy in a sixty-nine." Max focused his camera and adjusted his position to make room for the nine-inch hard-on that was coming to life at the mere thought of it. It was a beautiful sight watching the two women have sex. He'd always believed that most women were bi-curious, and the way these two went at it, he was certain of it. The Mitzy chick licked Charli like she was the last helping of a delectable dessert. Though Charli was more restrained, Mitzy's skilled efforts brought tears to her eyes. And he got it all on film. Let them try to prove this was doctored, he thought. Satisfied that he'd gotten the money shot, he put his camera down and unzipped his pants. Before he got his shirt off, Mitzy was gargling with his balls, and Charli had taken oral possession of his manhood.

It was fabulous watching that stuck-up Gillian—Charli—suck his dick like it was her last supper. After visiting the brink of orgasm more often than he could bear without losing it, he laid Charli down on the bed and spread her long, lean legs. She was wet and slick, thanks to Mitzy, who now held her sex open for all to see. Before he took her, he grabbed his camera and got a steamy shot of Mitzy holding Charli open in invitation. He was sure that Brandon would love *that* shot, in particular, his princess's treasured vault open for the masses to raid.

He put the camera down and slid all nine inches into her, stretching her tight wetness. He gave her strong, steady strokes, while Mitzy kissed first him and then Charli, all the while fondling his heavy balls.

While his right brain devoured the debauchery, his left brain decided that he wanted to always have access to Charli and her world of raunchy, hot sex that women like Lauren and her mother knew nothing about. There was nothing prim and proper about it, only primal, which most men understood fully. Having come to that conclusion he also came in her.

Chapter 23

A pall settled over the Russell estate after part two of the Gillian scandal shots was released. They spread through the media like a California wildfire, making the first set of shots look like a *Mary Poppins* photo shoot. There were close-ups, tongue-down-throat and tongue-up-twat shots that would have been virtually impossible to doctor, convincing many skeptics that the images were real. There were also no telltale signs of alteration, such as lack of symmetry or incongruent light reflections. The experts agreed that these shots had not been altered in any way.

The only person who could have imagined how an un-doctored shot that looked *exactly* like Gillian could not be her was Imelda, who you'd imagine would certainly remember carrying twins and giving one away, but *she* was not talking a lot lately. In fact, she was playing it very close to the vest after the uproar that ensued after Gillian discovered that her father was alive. For a minute she thought they were going to kick her out of the estate, but thankfully they hadn't.

The last few years hadn't been kind to the baroness. She'd always spent a lot of money baiting the hook for her next husband, including couture wardrobes from the Paris runways, first-class travel throughout the world, and the many other accoutrements necessary to lure and catch Mr. Big Bucks. She didn't mind at all, because her efforts had always reaped substantial rewards, that is, up until her last husband, the baron. Though he, too, had all of the trappings of great wealth, she discovered too late that he just didn't have the wealth itself. As a result, not only had she spent a fortune getting him to chase her, but she'd come up empty-handed. She'd tried to salvage the situation using what money she had left to find a runner-up, but so far, there were no takers. She was discovering that it was hard out there for an over-the-hill gold digger.

Imelda was another source of Brandon's disappointment with Gillian. When he first met his mother-in-law-to-be he thought she was a regal, rich, and worldly socialite, but over the last few weeks, he saw clearly that she was just an old, broke-ass hootchie looking for the next baller. The only difference between Imelda and a video ho was the stripper pole. After seeing her first husband on TV, he realized that she was no better than he was. She'd just cleaned up sooner and ran a little farther and a lot faster than he had after his own escape from the boonies.

Now he had to figure out how to get that woman out of his house, and decide whether he wanted her to take her slut daughter along with her. That, he knew, would depend on whether she brought home that Oscar, which he knew was now a long shot. If she didn't, she and her mother could both pack up and get the fuck out. He felt humiliated and conned after seeing the raunchy videos that had been sent to him personally. *Video* of his wife having sex with another man! Of course the bitch had the nerve to try and say that it wasn't her! Just like she said those photos weren't of her! What did he look like? Boo Boo the fool? All this time he thought he had married a lady who would help upgrade his image, but instead Gillian was nothing but a lying whore who'd used him to get ahead. He'd been played like a country fiddle, but that was all about to end, right along with her chances of winning the Oscar.

Rage boiled in his blood at the thought of her fucking another man. A man who hadn't spent the last three years giving her the world, and she still has the nerve to play him like a pussy. Obviously she didn't really know who she was dealing with. He might be all polished up, but the dirt and grit from the streets remained just beneath the surface.

Gillian was having a similar conversation in her head, though in her version leaving wasn't predicated on whether she won the Oscar. When all of this was over, she was leaving one way or the other. She'd been essentially numb since the latest shots were released, and the new video had her paralyzed with fear and confusion. They were all so real looking that for a split second she had to think about whether it was her!

To make matters worse, a few tabloids had picked up the thread of a rumor that surfaced right after Paulette was killed, and the media was having a field day speculating anew on suspects. Because she'd lived with Paulette before moving in with Brandon, someone with a wild imagination decided that they were lesbian lovers and that Paulette blackmailed her after she became famous, and that Gillian killed her to protect the secret. Now, of course, with pictures of her with another woman, they had "proof" that she was gay, so maybe she killed Paulette, too.

What bothered her most was the fact that her husband automatically believed what he saw, and probably what he heard as well. He had not once considered that she could be telling the truth. Since the photos were released, he'd looked at her like she was pond scum. They now slept in separate bedrooms.

Her mother, on the other hand, was uncharacteristically as quiet as a mouse. Gillian realized that Imelda felt bad about lying to her about her father and was trying to stay out of the way and not cause any more problems, but now was when she really needed to talk to someone, and with Reese consumed by Rowe's illness, she called Lauren overseas.

"Hi, it's me," she said.

The connection was bad, so she could barely hear Lauren. "Hi, Golden Girl," she said.

She was back in South Africa and had no idea what was going on in the tabloids back home. "Try Tarnished Girl instead," she said, wearily.

Even with a bad connection across continents, Lauren could hear the despair in her friend's voice. "What's wrong, sweetie?" she asked. She'd never heard Gillian sound so despondent before.

Gillian couldn't stop the flood of tears that came. She'd been holding so much in that it only took a kind and concerned voice to bring it all to the surface. After blowing her nose, she caught her breath and told Gillian everything that had happened.

"Oh my God, Gillian," she exclaimed. "You poor thing. That's awful."

"I swear it's not me."

"You don't even have to say that. We've just got to figure out who's behind this."

"I don't know how. My publicist has been working with a tech expert trying to trace the computer source through the Internet provider, but so far they've run into dead ends. And Brandon totally believes that I'm a whore who's tricked him into marriage."

"Forget about Brandon. Right now we need to focus on you. I have an idea. I'll take a flight out tomorrow and be in L.A. in a couple of days. Together, we'll get through this."

Gillian wanted to cry all over again—out of relief. Finally she'd have someone she could talk to, who was unconditionally on her side. "Lauren, you don't have to do this."

"There's no way I would let you go through this alone."

"You are a real friend," Gillian said, now fully appreciating the difference between friends and fauxs.

Chapter 24

Being fabulous was such hard work, Mildred lamented with a long, heartfelt sigh. She pressed the call button for her butler, James, for the second time. Where the hell was he when she needed him? He knew she was going shopping, and thus, should have expected she'd return with a barrage of shopping bags, therefore he should have been listening in eager anticipation for her arrival. Given the amount of staff she and Nathan employed, there was no reason she should ever be standing in the foyer of her home with armloads of shopping bags. Good help was *so* hard to find!

When James didn't materialize immediately, out of sheer frustration she resorted to an old-fashioned communication technique, and simply screamed out his name. "James, where are you?" she demanded, dropping the load of bags and her Birkin croc onto the foyer table and planting her hands on her hips.

Instead of James, Nathan entered the foyer along with a

woman whom she didn't recognize. "Mildred, you have company," he announced somewhat somberly.

In warp speed Mildred transformed from the spoiled, pissed-off bitch, to the cool and self-composed socialite that the rest of society saw and didn't necessarily like. "Hi, I'm Mildred Baines-Reynolds, and you are?"

"I'm Lydia, Lydia Patterson."

Mildred looked the homely woman up and down, deftly noting her Nine West shoes and the deplorable nondesigner suit she wore, stopping just short of turning up her chiseled nose. She abhorred tackiness on any level as though it were a contagious, rapidly spreading viral disease for which there was no vaccination or cure. "And what can I do for you?" Mildred fixed her with the same politely disdainful glare that she'd perfected on Paulette for so many years.

Knowing his wife all too well, Nathan interjected on the poor woman's behalf. "Ms. Patterson is with Celebrity Publishing and she's writing a book about Gillian and wanted a few quotes from us."

Lydia had purposefully waited until Mildred left for her shopping excursion and her scout reported that she was twenty minutes away from returning home before knocking on the door, knowing that she'd have a better chance of getting a foot into it if Nathan, rather than his famously prickly wife, answered it.

Mildred's next impulse was to show the mousy woman to the door, since she'd never thought very highly of Gillian and her kind, and was truly perplexed at how she'd attained such success *and* married such a very rich husband, when her own, more deserving daughter hadn't. Not to mention that people of her station in life dared not associate with the entertainment types, though it was different now that Gillian was an Oscar-nominated movie star, not one of those B-listers who showed up everywhere wearing as close to nothing as uncommon decency would allow. Then again, there were those pornographic pictures of her that everyone was talking about. So far, they'd only served to make her even more famous, so perhaps she should not be so hasty in judgment, since her affiliation would give her added cache among her catty friends, and they'd be *really* envious once she was invited to *Vanity Fair*'s famous Oscar party. My God, what would she wear? Hmmmm . . . There was that fabulous beaded gown she left hanging at Ralph Lauren's on Madison Avenue . . .

"Mrs. Baines-Reynolds?" Lydia said in an effort to return Mildred to the here and now. In those seconds, she'd gotten an unfiltered look at Mildred's self-absorption.

She knew that her journalistic skills would really come in handy during this process; in fact, they were part of the reason that she'd been successful as a publicist. Lydia had an uncanny ability to read the subtext in most any circumstance. Irrespective of what someone said, she usually saw the truth beyond the words. It was as clear to her as though teletype were scrolling across their faces. In this case, the teletype would have revealed Mildred's thoughts to be: 1) She's a nobody, maybe I should kick her out of my house; 2) And, she's writing a book about an actress; that could be tacky; 3) But, the actress is an A-list movie star, so perhaps I should hear her out; 4) Now that I think about it, this could be good for me.

"Yes, of course," Mildred said, snapping out of her reverie. "Would you care for something to drink?" Part three of her transformation was to that of the gracious hostess.

"I'd love something. Whatever you're having." Lydia smiled in her most disarming manner. She'd long figured out that she was far from a world-class beauty; in fact, she knew that looks were *not* her strong suit. She also knew how to work her unassuming qualities to her ultimate benefit, so she'd strategically left her Jimmy Choos and Armani suit hanging in the hotel room closet and thrown on a pair of just-purchased Nine West shoes, along with a getup she'd found at Ann Taylor. It was quite amazing how beautiful people discounted those who weren't as attractive, or rich.

Mildred led Lydia into the elegantly appointed sitting room, where James magically appeared. From where, she had no idea. "James, please bring a Glendronach single malt for Mr. Reynolds, and two glasses of the Boekenhoutskloof shiraz for my guest and I."

James scurried off to do her bidding, while Nathan sat opposite the chairs taken by Lydia and Mildred. Most of his days were excruciatingly boring, so he was very happy to have a splash of excitement in the midst of his normally benign existence.

"So tell me about this book," Mildred said.

"Well, as you know, the press and fans have been fascinated with Gillian Tillman-Russell. In fact, many in the industry expect her to be the next Grace Kelly, you know, an acclaimed movie star who is equally capable of transforming style . . ." Lydia rattled off more nonsense about Gillian, all in an effort to assure Mildred that the book she was working on was a positive cultural exploration rather than the tell-all, tabloidesque tome it was destined to be.

James arrived shortly, serving their drinks from an ornate ebony and platinum tray.

"So, what can I tell you?" Mildred asked, getting right to the point.

"You've known Gillian for years now, so what was she like, before becoming *the* Gillian Tillman-Russell?" Lydia asked, after taking a notepad and pen from her bag.

As Mildred talked, Lydia pretended to take detailed notes.

"Well, you know that she and my daughter, Lauren, are best friends," Mildred bragged.

"Yes, and I'm hoping to speak with Lauren when she returns to the States. Do you know when that might be?" Lydia's investigator told her that Lauren was in Cape Town, South Africa, with her boyfriend, a photographer named Gideon Gimble.

Mildred flushed a bit. She had no idea where Lauren was, nor when she might return. Lauren's late-found independent streak was quite unsettling to Mildred, who'd successfully manipulated every aspect of Lauren's entire life, including selecting her colleges, her majors, and, most notably, her hunky ex-hubby. And for her part, Lauren had been the dutiful daughter up until she met that bohemian photographer boyfriend of hers. It was like Lauren had an orgasm and lost her mind at the same time. Though Mildred certainly understood the power of great sex, she was also unwaveringly shrewd and calculatingly strategic when it came to self-preservation.

"Well, her plans keep changing, so I'm not sure exactly when Lauren will be stateside," Mildred answered coyly.

Lydia noted the hesitation. "So, tell me your impressions of Gillian?" she asked, changing the subject in an attempt to get Mildred comfortable and hopefully loose-lipped.

"She was quite a lovely girl," Mildred lied. Just as she didn't particularly care for Gillian, she didn't feel as if Gillian had ever shown her the deference to which she was entitled, either.

Lydia recognized a lukewarm endorsement when she heard one. "What about her husband, Brandon Russell?"

It was all Mildred could do not to turn up her nose this time. Even though the man certainly had tons of money, he was as nouveau and tacky as they came, perhaps surpassing dear deceased Paulette. "Seems to be a nice man," was her curt reply. *Lovely* and *nice* were both society code for "tolerable" and "barely tolerable."

"Though I'd rather not, in order to tell the complete story of Gillian's astronomical rise in Hollywood my publisher feels it's necessary to address the rumors that he might somehow have been involved in your niece's murder." Though detectives weren't able to tie their investigation of Brandon's money laundering to Paulette or her murder, there were rumblings in the PR world that Paulette might have found proof of Brandon's crimes.

Lydia also knew that Mildred had no lost love for Paulette, but she nonetheless screwed her face into a sad expression and said, "I know that you loved your niece and that this might be painful for you, but do you think Brandon could have had anything to do with her death?"

Mildred's equally phony expression conveyed deep concern and thoughtfulness. "I'd certainly hate to think that Gillian's husband would have had anything to do with Paulette's tragic death, but he *is* from the rap business," she said, as though this were irrefutable proof of latent murderous tendencies.

"That's a good point," Lydia said. Then she waited for more, realizing that Mildred was warming nicely to the topic at hand.

She didn't have to wait long.

"And from what I hear, he is the only person to have had access to the car to be able to cut the brake line. It would have been much harder for anyone else to sneak on to that guarded property and sabotage that car without being noticed," she pointed out. "And of course, Paulette was a very pushy . . . I mean persistent person, so assuming it's true that she had any incriminating evidence about Brandon's money laundering, she'd most certainly have blackmailed him, which would definitely be a compelling motive for murder." Mildred raised her immaculately coiffed eyebrows, hinting at her increasing level of suspicion. In one minute flat, Brandon had gone from a "nice man" to a derelict murderer. "Would you care for another glass of wine?" Mildred asked, mentally toasting a job very well done.

Chapter 25

Chris kept his prayer vigil at Rowe's side. Unlike Reese, he'd been praying all of his life and many of those prayers had been answered. He was a star athlete playing a sport he'd loved since he was Rowe's age and he made a lot of money doing it. Now if God could just bless him with one more answered prayer and do it quickly.

It seemed that every day Rowe was paler than the day before. He looked like a hollowed-out version of himself.

Kelly, one of the morning nurses, entered the room with the bright smile she always wore, irrespective of the often-gloomy tasks that her job demanded. "Good morning, Chris," she said, as she went about reading Rowe's chart.

"Not so sure about that," Chris answered.

"You've gotta have faith," she insisted, placing a hand on his arm.

"At this point, it seems that it may take a little more than faith to help my boy. He's not looking so good."

"Dr. Young has ordered a blood transfusion today. His red blood cells are pretty low, which is why he is so pale."

"When will he get it?" Chris asked, happy that at least something was happening to treat his son. The waiting game was getting old.

"As soon as we're sure that we have enough of his blood type."

Chris rolled up his sleeve. "No problem with that. Take mine. That's the least I can do since my bone marrow wasn't a match."

"No problem, I'll call the clinic to make arrangements," she said, absently picking up Rowe's chart again. She flipped a few pages, and asked, "What's your blood type?"

"It's O," Chris answered.

A frown appeared on her face. "Are you sure?"

"Positive. The team doctor drilled it into all of the players to know our types in the event of an accident. Why, is there a problem?"

A look of apprehension settled on Kelly's features and she put the chart back in the slot at the foot of Rowe's bed. "Umm, no, it's just that, uuhhm, you should speak to Dr. Young." She replaced the chart and was turning to leave, in a hurry.

Alarmed, Chris grabbed her arm. "What is wrong? Was there something in the chart? Is there a problem with my son?" he demanded.

The look of fear and concern on his face touched Kelly. She did not want to be the bearer of the information that she'd learned reading Rowe's charts, but neither could she leave him thinking that her concern was over his son's tenuous health. She lowered her head and her voice. "Rowe is AB, so there is no way that you could be a donor," she said.

"What do you mean? I'm his father," he said.

"Which means that you'd be either type A or B. Not O."

She saw the color drain from Chris's face, matching the sick pallor of the small child lying in the bed before him.

"I'm sorry," she said.

He wasn't sure how long he stood there wearing that blank, uncomprehending expression.

At some point, Kelly said, "You should sit down." After Chris sank into the chair, she walked quietly out of the room, deeply regretting that she'd told him such devastating news. But, given this process, it was likely that he would have found out eventually anyway, she only wished that it hadn't been on her watch.

Of all people, Chris knew what Reese was capable of; he'd experienced it firsthand. But he liked to think that that was the old Reese, before her brush with death.

He felt like such a sucker, because it had never even occurred to him—even when it became obvious to him and the whole world that she was an accomplished gold digger—that Reese would lie about Rowe's paternity. And now, with Rowe's life at stake, it sickened him to know that she would continue playing games that could cost her own son his life. What kind of person would do that, and more to the point, what kind of *mother* would do that?

Chapter 26

"You poor thing," Lauren said, as she hugged Gillian close and patted her back. "I am so sorry." She'd come over straight from the airport to comfort her best friend.

Gillian's tears kept coming. Lauren's comforting words and genuine concern allowed her to release the pent up angst over the state of her life. It was so ironic that just when she should have been on top of the world, she was in fact at her lowest point ever. She hadn't had anyone to lean on while her marriage was falling apart and her career was imploding during a public crucifixion. Her mother, who was too busy worrying about herself, was, of course, no comfort at all. And with Rowe's dire illness, Reese wasn't in the position to be concerned about much else, and the one person whom she should have been able to count on, her husband, was emotionally absent. They barely spoke to each other, only communicating about business through CoAnne.

"Why would anyone want to do this to me?" she asked.

Luckily Brandon was on a business trip in New York, and Imelda had checked herself into a medical center for a face-lift, so they had the whole house to themselves. They chose to have their pity party in Gillian's boudoir, her sanctuary. It was the only place in the house that she felt was truly her own.

"Unfortunately, sometimes it's the price you have to pay for fame."

"But it feels so personal, like someone deliberately wants to hurt me, rather than it being just a media ploy."

Lauren shrugged and added, "I know it's easier said than done but don't focus on it. The truth will come out and until then you just have to hold your head up high and keep moving forward, otherwise they win."

"I don't even want to be seen in public, I can't imagine doing the next round of media for the Oscar campaign. You know, every single reporter will ask me about those shots."

"Just follow the script that CoAnne gave you and never get off message."

"You know they've even thrown Paulette into this."

"What does Paulette have to do with nude pictures of you?" Lauren asked.

"Remember after the accident, when they were fishing for suspects everywhere? Since I had lived with Paulette, a rumor got out that we were lesbian lovers, and that after I became famous she blackmailed me, because I left her for Brandon. Because some of the photos show me—though it's not me—with another woman, people are now saying that it proves that I *am* a lesbian, and probably *was* Paulette's lover, and therefore, I must have killed her."

"You've got to be kidding!" Lauren said.

"I wish I were," Gillian said.

"There were some pretty flimsy motives tossed out back then—they accused just about everyone who'd ever known Paulette of killing her—but that one is ridiculous."

"I believe you were the only one of us that wasn't accused."

"Funny, huh, since I had more motive than anybody."

"Yeah, but you'd *just* found out about the affair and the baby minutes before the accident, so you wouldn't have had time to plan it. Speaking of suspects, where is Max?"

Lauren smirked and shook her head. "Last I heard he was down in Atlanta. Who knows what he's doing there since he can't practice law. You know he was disbarred after he and Paulette forged my grandmother's will."

"All of that seems like such a lifetime away," Gillian mused, and it was, she thought, Paulette's lifetime.

"How are things with Gideon?" she asked, finding a smile beneath her misery. It truly warmed her heart to see Lauren finally find herself and escape that manipulative mother of hers.

Lauren's face lit up despite the gloom of the evening. "Awesome!" Her smile spread from cheek to cheek. "He is *so* amazing. He's thoughtful, insightful, caring, smart, and so sexy . . ."

"Okay, okay," Gillian teased, holding up both hands in surrender. "I get it, he's perfect."

"I wouldn't go that far," Lauren laughed. "No man is, but he's as close to it as I can imagine."

"I am so happy for you." A pall came across Gillian's face as she remembered her and Brandon's engagement and wedding. She twisted the huge ring that sat like a giant boulder atop her finger.

Lauren grabbed her hand, knowing where her thoughts must have wandered.

"I should never have married Brandon," Gillian finally said.

"Don't beat yourself up. I could say the same thing about Max. You live and you learn."

Gillian looked up at Lauren and took a cleansing breath; she was finally ready to make a confession about something that had been weighing on her heart and soul since right after Paulette's death. "Lauren, I have something to tell you that I'm not proud of, and that I've never told anyone else."

Her serious tone scared Lauren, who couldn't imagine anything worse than what had already happened to her. "What is it, honey?"

Gillian lowered her head in shame as she took another deep breath, steeling herself to say the words she thought she never could. "I have proof that Paulette discovered that Brandon had been laundering money just as the feds suspected, and that she was blackmailing him. In other words, he really did have a serious motive for killing her."

Lauren was stunned. "What? Are you kidding?"

"No. Remember, I met Brandon after our luggage was

mixed up on my flight from JFK to LAX. I was living with Paulette at the time, and she must have gone through his things and found the flash drive with evidence on it and decided to keep it. After Brandon and I started dating, he asked me several times if I had seen it in his luggage, and I told him that I hadn't. He then asked if Paulette had been alone with his bag and of course she had, so I asked her about it and she denied knowing anything about it, and I told him that."

"What was on the drive?"

"Brandon told me that the drive proved that he didn't do it, and he was worried that the feds would get their hands on it and destroy it, but it actually contained a double set of accounting records, proving that he *had* laundered money, which is why he was so desperate to get it back."

"How did you get it?"

"Remember after Reese got out of the hospital, when we took her back to Paulette's apartment in New York to get her things? She found an envelope with Brandon's name on it in Paulette's safe deposit box and gave it to me. I was so excited when I saw it, thinking that it would clear his name, but when I looked at it, I realized that it would actually incriminate him. I should have never accepted his proposal and given it to the police, especially since they'd questioned him about her murder, but I didn't. I realized that if he went to jail, *Gold Diggers* wouldn't be finished and my career would be over before it started. I'm so sorry." Her eyes pleaded with Lauren for forgiveness and understanding. "Even though I had proof that he was a money launderer, I didn't want to believe that he could actually be a murderer."

"Just because Paulette had the drive still doesn't mean that he had anything to do with her death." Lauren was struggling to understand all of this. After Paulette's death, she'd left the country with Gideon and had been traveling the world ever since, anxious to put all of it—Paulette, Max, her mother, and the murder—behind her.

"That's not all that was in the envelope," Gillian said. "There was also a copy of a letter written by Paulette to Brandon blackmailing him."

Lauren hung her head. "Oh, no!"

"You know that Paulette was fixated on power, and holding something over someone like Brandon gave her more of it."

"Do you really think he killed her?" Now Lauren was concerned. She was concerned for Gillian's safety. If Brandon killed once to protect a secret, there was no reason he wouldn't do it again.

"When I first read the note and saw what was on the drive, my impulse was that he must have killed her, but I quickly talked myself out of believing it." She remembered standing in the office and hearing Brandon enter the house. She had only seconds to decide what to do with the drive she was holding, to decide whether to give it to him and pretend not to know what was on it, or to confront him about what he'd done and let the chips fall where they may. In the end, she froze and did neither.

That same night he proposed to her. She slipped the disk in her pants pocket, buried her head in the sand, and said, 'Yes." Gillian desperately wished that she could go back to that moment and make a different decision.

"He was offering me the world, not to mention the career that I'd always dreamed of, so I didn't even tell him that I had it. I'd like to think that fame and fortune wouldn't have made me turn my back on finding Paulette's killer, if I'd *really* known he'd done it, but honestly, based on how I behaved, I'm not so sure." Again, tears rolled down her cheeks. Gillian had carried that shame with her every day and it made the brightest moments dark, and the darkest moments unbearable. She buried her face in her hands and sobbed, for Paulette and for herself.

After Gillian managed to compose herself, Lauren asked, "Where is the drive now?"

"It's hidden in a pair of Manolo boots; the last place that Brandon would ever have cause to look."

"Did you make a copy?"

"No."

"We need to do that right now," Lauren insisted.

Gillian nodded. "You're right." She immediately got up and walked over to her wall of shoes, wondering why she hadn't thought to do this herself. She climbed up the stepladder and reached for a box at the very top. After sitting back down with the box between them, she opened it and felt in the toe of one of the black suede boots. When she didn't feel anything, she reached into the other one, but, to her shock and dismay, nothing was there either. Someone had stolen the flash drive along with the blackmail note. "Oh, my God!" Gillian exclaimed.

"What's wrong?" Lauren asked, reading the look of fear on Gillian's face.

"It's gone. Someone's stolen the evidence."

Chapter 27

Lydia had spent the preceding days having her hair extended, cut, colored, and styled, her skin exfoliated and Botoxed, and her body tanned, buffed, and massaged, all in preparation for her press announcement of *Lights, Cameras, and Action! The Story of Fame, Fortune, and Fatality.*

Working with her publisher's publicist they'd arranged a news conference and invited more than thirty media outlets, from *USA Today* and the *Enquirer,* to *Entertainment Tonight* and CNN. The turnout was spectacular. They all smelled blood amid the scintillating story of glamour, sex, celebrity, betrayal, and money. And the timing couldn't be better with the Academy Awards now only six weeks away, and the media whipped into a frothy frenzy over Gillian's photo escapades.

"Thanks for coming," the publicist said to the crowd of bloodthirsty press hounds. "Lydia Patterson will read the press release and then take a few questions."

Though Lydia had been involved in lots of press conferences in her life, this was the first time she was on the other side of the podium. Nervous, but excited, she stepped up to the mike. She'd spent days employing every beauty trick she'd ever heard about, and hours trying on outfit after outfit, but she still looked, well, mousy. All of the money, pampering, and designer garb in the world would only do so much for her. She was a glamour girl trapped in and desperately trying to get out of a librarian's body. It was true, you couldn't make silk from a sow's ear, or to paraphrase President Obama, a pig wearing lipstick was still just a pig.

"Thank you all for coming," she started. "As you read in the prerelease, *Lights, Cameras, and Action! The Story of Fame, Fortune, and Fatality* is a biography of the titillating, and often calculating, life of Gillian Tillman-Russell. As most of you know, I worked for Mr. and Mrs. Russell for a couple of years and felt that her story was important enough to write about for several reasons. First, I hope that it will paint a real picture of someone who is relatively new to the public but who has also captured their imagination like no one in recent memory. Second, I wanted to explore how she became who she is. Hers is an exciting, but cautionary, tale of fame, fortune, and the fast lane. Third, as you all know, several years ago, one of Gillian's best friends, and a friend to many of us, the publicist Paulette Dolliver, was murdered in a tragic car accident off of Mulholland Drive. You may also remember that Gillian's husband, Brandon Russell, who was being investigated by the federal government for money laundering at the time, was considered a suspect. In this book I also explore that connection and how it relates to who the real Gillian Tillman-Russell is. The exotic beauty we're all getting to know, or the tantalizing temptress shown in the barrage of recent sex photos, whose legitimacy she refutes?" Lydia ended with her cliff-hanger.

After letting the toxins soak into the room she added, "My publisher and I expect the book to be released the week of the Oscars. Thank you all for your time."

Before she finished the word *time*, cameras were flashing like fireflies, hands were raised one after the other, and her name was being shouted out by reporters anxious to ask her questions. It was the moment she'd dreamed of, being the center of attention, a star, and a celebrity in her own right, and she *loved* every minute of it.

"Lydia, Lydia. Does the book prove that the pictures are real?" a reporter from the *Enquirer* asked.

"She denies that the photos are real, but our forensic experts conclude that they have not been altered in any way. And yes, we will provide the evidence in the book."

"Do you delve into her mother's past?"

"In the book, I chronicle Imelda von Glich's journey from Waynesboro, North Carolina, to European royalty, all courtesy of one rich husband being followed by an even richer one. As a journalist, I'm not passing judgment, and only point it out because *Gold Diggers* also happens to be the title of the film for which Gillian is nominated for an Oscar. Next question."

A *New York Post* reporter asked the million-dollar question. "Did Brandon Russell really kill Paulette and was Gillian complicit in it?"

This was what most of those gathered here really wanted to know. Lydia had consulted with her publicist, her lawyers, as well as her publisher, to make sure that she gave an answer that would entice the media without overpromising or baiting a lawsuit, so she said, "My investigation has uncovered new evidence that the authorities will have to evaluate to make that determination."

The room erupted into unbridled chaos! The press became ravenous as everyone gathered anticipated the serving of a blockbuster news-breaking story, which would feed lots of news pages and consume tons of airtime. It was nothing short of thrilling for members of the media and simply orgasmic for Lydia. At that moment, the publicist stepped forward and ended the press conference. They'd all agreed to end on that prickly but pivotal question. Always leave them wanting more was Lydia's motto.

Brandon sat in his office unable to move for several minutes. The rapid-fire thoughts that ricocheted through his mind had simply shorted a circuit. He was unsure which emotion or issue to deal with first. He felt pissed off, betrayed, and afraid, and had to think about what to do to resolve each. His phone began ringing immediately. Though he didn't answer any of the calls, caller ID informed him that among others, he'd received calls from the press, his attorney, various colleagues, family members, a few friends, and even a few fauxs.

Still in a stupor, he got up and went to the wet bar, and poured himself a double shot of Louis XV to steady his nerves. Over the last few years he'd allowed himself to believe that the money laundering charges were behind him. Even though he hadn't gotten the flash drive from Paulette before she died, he still chose to believe that the loose end had died right along with her. He'd hoped that she'd had it in her bag and that it, along with much of the car, had gone up in smoke. Now he couldn't help but think that Lydia had it, otherwise what new evidence could there be that would implicate him? But how could Lydia have gotten her hands on it?

Out of nowhere a snatch of a conversation replayed itself. It happened shortly after Paulette's death when Reese returned to L.A. from New York. She came by the house one day, and Brandon saw her briefly before Gillian came down. She'd asked him if he'd received the package. Before he could ask what package, Gillian walked in and quickly said, "Reese, darling, it was supposed to be a surprise." He could feel a session of mental telepathy playing out between the two friends.

Later on, Gillian explained that she'd talked to Reese about ordering a Loro Piana cashmere bathrobe for him and that's the package she was referring to. Sure enough, a week later one did arrive in the mail. But now he was wondering if maybe Reese had found the drive among Paulette's things and sent it to him through Gillian. Then, of course, Lydia could have taken it from his wife.

He was beginning to wonder if he'd ever really known Gillian at all. In retrospect, she seemed to be quite capable of deception and duplicity, but then again, she was an actress, wasn't she?

Chapter 28

Even though Rowe was not as pale as before the blood transfusion, he was still extremely weak, and so far, there wasn't a bone marrow match in sight, and time was slipping by. On Reese's more morbid days, she imagined that she could actually see his life also slipping away. Reese had never felt more powerless, and utterly unable to do anything to help the son for whom she'd vowed to do anything.

"Mommy, am I gonna die?" he asked, wearing a solemn expression that was way beyond his tender years. Over the weeks Rowe had grasped the gravity of his situation from the sad-faced adults who hovered around his bed.

"Of course not, baby. You're gonna be fine. Dr. Young, me, and your dad are gonna make sure of it."

Reese only wished that she felt as certain as her answer. In truth she felt helpless, so at his bedside, she did all that she could, which was limited to holding his hand, rubbing his head, and continuing to pray for that miracle that so far had evaded her. When she was honest with herself she was forced to admit that there was something else that she could do for Rowe.

She could face up to her past, try to contact Rowe's real father, and let the chips fall where they may. Testing him for bone marrow matching was probably Rowe's best chance of survival, given the tight timing and the randomness of the national database search. That plan seemed easy enough, but in her world nothing was ever so simple. Reese felt as if she were on the receiving end of one of God's most outlandish jokes, only Rowe was the punch line, and there was nothing funny about it.

She only wished that that one drunken encounter had never happened. They had been sober enough to slap on a condom, but when it was over, they both realized that it had burst.

In an effort to seal the deal with Chris, Reese had been flushing her birth control pills down the drain for months, secretly trying to get pregnant. So when the home test finally read positive, she jumped for joy and didn't give another thought to the broken condom. Her mission had been accomplished. She and Chris were married a month later.

The all too familiar trip to and from the hospital was beginning to be a grind. She left the house every morning praying and hopeful that somehow Rowe's condition had improved and that Dr. Young had been wrong all along and that she could bring her son home. Yet each night she returned home alone to face the dire fact that he wasn't miraculously getting better, and, in fact, was getting worse.

She parked the car and dragged herself into the house, ready to collapse into her bed, so that she could wake up and do the same thing the next day.

"Any update?"

Reese turned around and was surprised to find Chris entering the hallway from the living room. If she had not been so preoccupied she probably would have noted the clench in his jaw; a definite warning sign.

"I didn't know you were here."

"Gretchen let me in," he said. "So, what's up?"

"No change, really." She dropped her bag on the side table and headed toward the kitchen, hoping that Chris wouldn't get settled and would leave soon. She had been trying to avoid him since he came to town, figuring that the less they saw of each other, the better the chances that her secret would remain just that.

"Are you sure about that?" Chris asked, following behind her, barely managing to hold back the rage that had been mounting within him for two days now. The day after learning that he wasn't Rowe's father, he holed up at the Four Seasons to avoid the risk of running into Reese at the hospital. He knew that he couldn't be responsible for what might have happened, and he didn't want that negative energy anywhere near Rowe.

Reese kept walking toward the kitchen and responded to Chris without turning around to face him. "The blood transfusion helped, but without a bone marrow transplant Dr. Young doesn't expect much change, at least not for the better."

"Then why don't you do what any responsible mother would do and have his *real* father tested instead of playing this game of Russian roulette with your son's life?"

Reese stopped in her tracks. Her old and tried survival instincts told her to lie and deny, but her better instincts told her that those tired tactics would only make matters worse.

Chris walked around to face her. "You don't have anything to say?" Though he hadn't raised his voice yet, his anger was loud and clear.

"Chris, I'm sorry," Reese said, lowering her head. Nothing in her life of winning at all costs prepared her for this stark moment of truth.

"Is that it?" he asked, his arms outstretched, his brows raised in disgusted disbelief. Heat rose from his face as blood cursed through his veins, spreading the raging anger that was becoming uncontrollable. "After lying to me and Rowe for all of these years, even marrying me so that you wouldn't have a 'bastard child' when it wasn't even mine! As if that's not enough, you've cashed my very generous child support checks every month for over two years, knowing that I was supporting another man's child." He shook his head in disbelief. "But you wanna know what's worse than all of that? The fact that you are so *fucking* selfish that you won't even tell the truth to save your own child's life. I'm sure for fear of losing the only thing you've ever really cared anything about: the almighty dollar." He looked at Reese as if she were the lowest form of specimen to ever slither the earth. "You disgust me," he finally said, as he turned to walk away.

When the door slammed shut, and the reverberations

subsided, tears began a slow, familiar trek down Reese's face. She felt like the same desperate eighteen-year-old from Queens who'd plotted and planned her way into becoming an NBA wife.

After the car accident, Reese had wanted to change, and had tried very hard to make up for some of the damage that she'd done to herself and to others, knowing that some things could never be repaired. Her biggest regrets were not being a better mother to Rowe before the accident, using Chris for his money and status, and then trashing him in the divorce for even more of his money. To make up for those sins, she'd embraced her son and become a better mother, but she still wasn't putting him ahead of her own needs, otherwise she'd have started searching for his real father right away. As much as she wanted to face up to her responsibility and do the right thing by her son, she also wondered if she and others she cared about could survive the fallout once Rowe's father's true identity was known.

Though her stripes were a little different, Reese realized that old habits died hard, and that she was still the same old gold digger that she had been three years ago.

Chapter 29

"My God, the wicked things you do to me!" Mildred panted, breathlessly. As always, Max left her feeling completely and lasciviously ravished. Being the controlling person that she was, she loved the chance to let go and be dominated by a strong, sexy man. It was just unfortunate that it wasn't her husband doing it, and even less fortunate that this man who did was her own daughter's ex-husband. Yet she still flushed like a hormonal teenager whenever she thought back to the day they met, eight years ago.

It was early June and Lauren had just graduated from Harvard. After the ceremony Lauren and Nathan left for New York, while Mildred headed to the house in Martha's Vineyard to check on renovations. Before she got there, her rental car sputtered to a stop along a deserted road. Truly exasperated at both her butler and her husband for not figuring out how to refuel her rented car's tank mid-trip and across state lines, she got out of the car, put one hand firmly on her hip, whipped out her cell phone with the other, then prepared to read someone the riot act, but before she could press send a silver Lamborghini cruised to a stop right along-side her incapacitated convertible.

Inside sat a man straight out of a Dolce & Gabbana ad. His creamy complexion, kissed and then licked by the sun, glowed magnificently, and his teeth flashed whiter than freshly whipped cream. He was so attractive that Mildred immediately snapped her phone shut before he ever said one word.

"It looks like you could use a hand," he said smiling broadly.

"Maybe I could," Mildred tossed right back at him. Her flirt gene kicked in hard after years of dormancy. It mattered not that the sexy man in front of her was young enough to be her son.

"I'll pull over and see what I can do for you." He all but winked, so confident was this man in his proven ability to melt the hearts, minds, and panties of the opposite sex.

His engine purred to a stop in front of her car, and he hopped out and strolled directly up to her, stopping merely inches away. "So, what can I do for you?" he asked, sugges-tively, wielding that seductive smile like a black belt.

The sexual energy was so intense that Mildred's breath came in quick fits and slow starts. She took a deep one and answered, "I seem to have run out of gas."

"I think I can take care of that." Ever cocky, he closed the few inches between them, held her face in his hands, and introduced his lips to hers as if administering life support. It was love at first suck. They locked in an embrace that left Mildred panting for more.

He pulled her into the woods just off the road, backing her up against a large sycamore tree before turning her around and pulling up her delicately laced sundress. Before she could protest—not that she really would have—he was balls deep inside of her, and she was making sure he stayed there.

Up until that moment, Mildred had only known the kind of perfunctory sex necessary to get married and have babies, and had believed it was overrated and that a female orgasm was about as real as the Loch Ness monster; an insidious myth perpetuated over time to ensure the population of the planet Earth. So, she was turned inside out well before he laid her on the ground and tried to plow through to China.

When he finally rolled off, she turned to him and purred, "Who are you?" as though he were an action hero in a Hollywood thriller.

"I'm Max," he said, zipping up his pants. "Maximillian Neuman, the Third."

Here they were eight years, two marriages, and one death later, still hot and heavy as ever. She reached over and massaged him lovingly, enjoying his weight and girth. With Nate away and the staff dismissed for the rest of the day, she relished the long, sweet afternoon to come and come, and come . . . They'd polished off a bottle of Krug and were working on the second. There was no rush. She took a swallow and held it in her mouth, before slithering southward where she consumed him right along with the fine bubbly. It was now time for round two.

He grew in size appreciably and began moving his hips urgently to meet her lips. Grabbing the back of her head, he groaned in ecstasy, thrust himself unrelentingly in and out of her mouth. Max took her mouth as forcefully as he had taken her sex only moments earlier, though there were no signs of complaint. Mildred had her eyes shut and her mouth stuffed wide open, full of Max's penis.

The debauched lovers had no idea that footsteps had fallen outside of their lair. Just as Max groaned lewdly and climaxed thoroughly, the door began to ease open, unveiling to Lauren the shock of her life.

She was way beyond speechless at the improbable sight of her proper, etiquette-conscious mother butt naked with her slimy ex-husband's engorged dick stuffed like pork sausage down her throat. She slowly backed away, thinking, No, no, it can't be. She simply couldn't believe what she had just seen with her very own eyes.

Chapter 30

Lauren lay on her bed in the Gansevoort Hotel with a towel pressed to her head and a million horrifying, dizzying, preposterous, insane thoughts racing through her mind, ransacking her brain. How could her mother, her über proper, socialite mother, possibly be fucking *anybody*, let alone Lauren's own slimy *ex*-husband? And how long had this sordid affair been going on? She leaned over to her side, toward the garbage can she'd left there, as another wave of nausea churned her stomach. The mere thought of them having sex was disgusting, but the visual had proven enough to literally turn her stomach.

She'd left L.A. feeling bad that Gillian did not have a supportive family to lean on at a point when she needed one most. Since she was seeing her stateside doctors in New York for checkups while in the country, she decided to bury the hatchet and surprise her own parents by spending a couple of days with them before heading back out of the country. She had decided to reestablish her relationship with her mom, but on her own terms. Lauren had no idea that *she'd* be the one in for the big surprise. She remembered being young and not being able to even imagine her mother having sex at all, even with her father, so the notion of her carrying on a torrid, salacious affair with Max, in her own marital bed, was completely unfathomable.

"We are so good together," she'd heard her mother say. Her speech had been a little slurred; Lauren wasn't sure if it was from physical overexertion, oral lubricant, or the two bottles of Champagne she'd seen littering the bedside table. As outlandish as this was, on one level it made picture-perfect sense. When she and Max were married, and Mildred was all up in the middle of their business about having a baby, she recalled cynically wondering why her mother didn't just fuck Max for her and get it over with. She'd mused that if she did, her mother would probably get pregnant and happily give birth to her own grandchild. The thought was in jest; little did she know just how close to the truth it was.

"We've always been good together. Since that day eight years ago when I found you stranded on the side of the road," Max said, in that smarmy tone he used when he was being charming to get his way. Though it was a wasted effort today since it looked as though he was getting exactly what he wanted, no questions asked.

Lauren's knees nearly buckled when she heard his statement. Her mother and Max had been having an affair for eight years! Before she had even met him. Their whole relationship and marriage—which Mildred pushed—was nothing more than a sick, elaborate ruse so that they could keep fucking without drawing suspicion. Lauren had leaned back against the wall; she was so dizzy that she'd nearly dropped her iPhone and the bouquet of roses she'd brought as a peace offering to her mother, whose voice interrupted her thoughts.

"Who else are you good with these days, now that you're hanging out in Atlanta where I can't keep my eyes on you?"

Lauren could hear a whisper of jealousy, along with the effects of the alcohol, in her mother's voice.

"What makes you think I'm with anybody else? You know how I feel about you."

"Because I know you," Mildred retorted sharply. "Besides, remember Paulette and that mess I had to clean up?"

"What do you mean *you* cleaned up?" Max asked. "As I recall, we both took care of that problem."

"You know what I mean," Mildred said. "If it weren't for my influence with the attorney general you surely would have been arrested for her murder."

"Probably so. But we couldn't have me going to jail, now, could we?" A scintilla of threat laced his tone.

Lauren could hear the bed linen rustle.

"Maybe not for murder, that wouldn't be good, but maybe I should have pressed charges when you and that little slut-niece of mine messed with the will," she teased.

"I told you I didn't know that Priscilla's signature was forged," he insisted. Paulette and Max, who was then the family attorney, had conspired, after her grandmother Priscilla's death, to forge the will to make sure that Paulette was at least redeemed financially after years of being the poor relation. At first Max was reluctant, but by the time Paulette held up the stick, by reminding him that she might slip and reveal their affair, and then dangled the carrot, that she'd share a percent with him, it was all but done.

"Who do you think you're fooling?"

"I don't know what the problem is; you got the money back when Paulette was killed."

"Yes, I did," she said, suddenly sounding very sober. "Yes, I did."

A dark chill coursed through Lauren's veins as she recalled the callous way in which the two lovers discussed the cold-blooded murder of an ex-lover and niece. Lauren's concerns about her mother now ran far deeper than who she was fucking, to the much more insidious question of whether she was capable of murder. If asked the same question only a day before, Lauren would have said unequivocally no, but that was before catching her mother in the middle of a bacchanalian fuck-fest with her own son-in-law and her daughter's ex-husband.

Chapter 31

The next day, Mildred was as content as a fat cat with a belly full of nice warm cream. Nathan was still out of town and Max was still in town, which meant she'd have a few more days to enjoy his many skills.

She was sprawled out on her chaise with her morning tray of Illy French-pressed coffee, freshly squeezed orange juice, a bagel with lox and cream cheese, along with a bowl of fruit. To her left sat the *New York Times*, the *Post*, and her MacBook Air laptop. Life was good, and getting better by the day.

Checking her e-mail, she opened a link sent by one of her friends entitled "More nude photos of Gillian Tillman-Russell." She could not say that she felt sorry for the girl; after all, she always had been such an uppity little bitch, which Mildred could never understand, given the fact that she had no pedigree whatsoever. Her mother was a gold-digging tramp and her father, we all now knew, was a backwoods country bumpkin.

She took a sip of her coffee and clicked on one of the images, settling in for a few minutes of entertainment. Ummm, so, Gillian was quite the busy girl. These photos showed her actually having sex with a man who certainly was not that little imp Brandon Russell. The mystery man's face was never shown, but being the connoisseur she was she could nonetheless see that he was a fine specimen. He seemed to be quite tall with a light caramel complexion, a nice body, and a rather distinctive mole on his hip . . . ?

She looked closer, zooming in on one of the shots and realized that she had seen that mole before, up close and personal, just yesterday! "That sneaky, cheating motherfucker!" she spewed, not realizing the accuracy of her unintended double entendre.

"Madam, is everything okay?" Hearing the commotion, James appeared at her side ready to handle any impending crisis.

"Go away, James," she commanded. Where was the inept little man when she really needed him, she thought, bitterly. She had to take her rage out on someone and he was the only person handy.

He tucked his tail and slinked backward out of the room.

That no good, slimy little fuck! she fumed. Who the hell *hadn't* he fucked? By her count alone she tallied her daughter, her niece, herself, and now her daughter's best friend, the double-crossing little bitch.

While Lauren had practically exiled her—for what she didn't know—Mildred did know that her daughter had embraced Gillian as her surrogate family. Just wait until she told Lauren that her Miss Goody Two-Shoes friend was fucking her husband. That should do it.

But wait, how could she tell Lauren that the naked, face-less man in the photograph was Max, without admitting that she'd fucked him herself? Her devious and nimble mind got to work and soon came up with a solution to her sticky little problem. She'd say that she recalled seeing Max in Speedos in Martha's Vineyard and noticed the mole. Then, surely, Lauren would see the similarities since in theory she should know her ex-husband's body better than Mildred did. Mil-dred only needed to plant the poisonous seed in Lauren's head, and then sit back and watch it grow.

Now that she had a plan, she felt better. She reached for the phone and dialed Lauren's international cell phone number, hoping that she'd pick up and not be forced to leave yet another voice mail message. This information needed to be imparted in conversation, not via voice mail. To her sur-prise, on the third ring Lauren did pick up.

"Hello?" She sounded as if she was right next door, rather than who knew where in the world.

"Hi, darling, it's your mother." Mildred had summoned a warm, loving tone with which to deliver her verbal blows. "How are you? In fact, where are you?"

There was a knock at her bedroom door. Annoyed, she said, "Just a minute, sweetie." She covered the receiver and shouted, "What do you want, James?"

"It's me, mother," Lauren answered, as she walked into the room and snapped her cell phone shut.

Mildred's eyes lit up in surprise. She had no idea that Lauren was even on the continent, let alone in Westchester, New York! She hopped out of the chaise and ran over to hug her daughter, whom she hadn't seen in many months. When she hugged Lauren she noticed that Lauren didn't quite hug her back. Oh well, she still had a little attitude, but that would end when Mildred told her what a traitor her best friend was. Then Lauren would once again cling to her for advice, rather than that devious little cunt Gillian.

She stood away from Lauren still holding her shoulders appraisingly. "It's so good to see you, and you look great!" And she did, Mildred thought. Aside from the fact that she was glowing and looked radiantly tanned, there was something more mature about her. Obviously running around the world with that bohemian artist agreed with her, or more likely it was the sex.

"Thanks, Mother."

"Please, have a seat," Mildred said, gesturing to two chairs that sat nestled in the bay window of her apartment-sized bedroom. "This is such a pleasant surprise. So, tell me, what brings you to the States and here? And why didn't you call me? I would have had your room ready."

"I won't be staying long," Lauren said. "I'm on the way from L.A. back to South Africa."

"L.A.? Visiting Gillian?" Here was her opening, Mildred thought.

"Yes, she's going through a bad time, as you probably know."

"Yes, I do," Mildred answered, adopting a very concerned demeanor. "In fact, I was just sent a link this morning with more of those horrible nude photos. As I was looking at them, a mole on the man's left hip caught my eye, and, I know this is going to sound crazy, but I flashed on an image of Max at Martha's Vineyard one summer wearing those little Speedo swim trunks, and he had the exact same heart-shaped mole." She hopped up and grabbed her laptop to show the evidence to Lauren.

After looking at the picture, Lauren's mouth hung open in shock. The man's body did in fact look like Max's.

Misreading her reaction, Mildred leaned over and held Lauren's hand and said, "Honey, I'm so sorry. I thought this was Max."

"You should know," Lauren said evenly, though her eyes cut right through the smoke and mirrors that Mildred hid behind.

"Whatever are you talking about?"

"Don't play games with me, Mother," Lauren snapped.

"It seems to me that your dear friend Gillian is the one playing games."

"Playing games is one thing, but sleeping with my ex-husband—your own son-in-law—is just plain sick!"

"If I'm not mistaken this photo clearly shows Gillian having sex with Max. Not me."

Lauren flipped open her cell phone and said, "And *this* photo clearly shows *you* fucking Max." There it was, the photo that Lauren snapped through a crack in the door before sneaking out of the house the day before.

What color there was in Mildred's yellow complexion ebbed away. And the shock took her breath away, right along with the ready recitation of lies. Though she and Max had been carrying on their affair for years now, she'd long since stopped worrying about getting caught. The euphoria of the sex had desensitized her to the reality of what she was truly doing and the huge risks that were involved. Besides the deep humiliation, ever the narcissist, she was also embarrassed because the photo was not a very flattering shot of her. Lauren definitely caught her bad side.

"Lauren, I'm sorry, it's not what you think . . . I didn't . . . It was . . ." She really couldn't think of anything to say and babbled just to try and control the situation.

Lauren stood up and slung her bag over her shoulder. "Mom, cut the crap, okay? It all makes perfect sense. Now I know why you pressured me to marry that louse, so that you could have your little fuck-buddy close by and on call. You used me to satisfy your own sick perversion."

"Lauren, it wasn't like that. Please try to understand." By now, all pretenses were dropped and the great Mildred was reduced to tears as she pleaded for understanding.

"Oh, I understand all right. I understand that you weren't just pissed with Paulette for having an affair and a baby by my husband, you were more ticked off that she took your toy."

"No!"

"I think so. I think that Paulette probably found out your little secret and to solve all three problems you and Max killed her."

"That's not true! I would never do that. You have to believe me."

"I can't say that I do, since, before yesterday, I wouldn't have thought you'd fuck my husband either." Lauren looked at Mildred with disdain, shook her head in disgust, and walked out the door.

Chapter 32

Two days had passed, and Reese still felt the anger and finality that resonated as Chris slammed the door shut and stormed out of her life. But those aftershocks were nothing compared to the earth-shattering, gut-wrenching blow to the gut that she felt when Dr. Young called to say that Rowe's condition was worsening.

After finally experiencing unconditional love, the thought of losing her precious son was like having her heart snatched right out of her chest. Love had been only an abstract term for Reese until after the car accident when Rowe stood vigilantly at her bedside at a time when she wasn't sure there was much to live for. His unshakable love was a soothing balm that healed her heart; her body and her soul soon followed. Little Rowe held her hand and told her over and over again that he loved her, and that she was still the most beautiful mother in the world, regardless of the bloodied bandages, broken bones, and skin that was marred black and blue, nowhere near her legendary sex-kitten image. He told her that she had to come home soon so that he could show her his new computer. He'd just learned his colors and numbers and couldn't wait to show off to his mother, whom he'd loved even when she was only a distant, glamorous figure in his life. Now the tables were turned. He was the one lying in the hospital bed clinging to life, yet there was nothing that she could do to save him.

"Honey, you've got to be strong. Losing it will not help Rowe," Gillian said. "Here, let me have Gretchen fix us some tea." Reese had called her an hour ago sounding very upset, so Gillian had raced right over to be with her friend.

After instructing Gretchen, Gillian led Reese to the sitting room off of her master suite.

"So, tell me what's happened?" Gillian asked.

"Everything has gone all wrong, and it's all my fault."

"Reese, tell me exactly what's going on," she insisted, handing Reese a tissue.

"Dr. Young called this morning. Rowe's white blood count is looking pretty bad, and he has another fever." A fresh set of tears flowed, taking her breath away.

Gillian remained cool, realizing that she had to counter Reese's emotions in order to be of help to her and her son. "Still no luck with a bone marrow match?"

Reese sniffled and wiped her nose. "No."

"What about his real father, Reese? It's time to stop playing games. Your son's life is at stake here."

Reese took a deep breath. "I don't know where he is," she said, shaking her head.

"Do you know *who* he is?" She had to ask that question,

after all, they were talking about Reese during her hard partying days.

Reese shot her a look. "Of course I do."

"So that means we can find him."

Reese lowered her head in defeat. "It's not that easy."

"Who is he?" Gillian finally asked.

When Reese's only response was to wring her hands and
bite her lips, Gillian stood up and grabbed her by the shoulders and gently shook her. "Are you listening to me? This
could be the last chance you have to save your son. Who is
his father?"

"You are going to hate me," Reese said in a small voice
as fresh tears trailed her cheeks.

"Reese, none of us is perfect, so don't worry about being judged, just worry about your son."

"If only it were so simple."

"Reese, I'm going to ask you one more time. If you don't
answer you're on your own here. I can't help you if you don't
come clean, so for the last time, who is Rowe's father?"

Reese sighed and let go of the deep dark secret she'd
held tight for so long. "It's Max. Max is Rowe's father."

"Oh, shit." The words just came out of Gillian's mouth
unbidden, as she sank onto the sofa, in stunned disbelief.

"I know. It's fucked up. Lauren is going to kill me."

"Honey, after his shenanigans with Paulette, I don't
think Lauren will be too surprised or really care. The man is
a whore."

"So what does that make me?" A tired smile crept across
her face.

"I refuse to judge you."

"It only happened once." Reese shrugged. "We were both drunk one night and ran into each other at the bar at the Four Seasons. One thing led to another, and from there upstairs to a hotel room.

"The next morning when I was sober, I immediately regretted it. To be honest, when I found out that I was pregnant, it really didn't cross my mind that the baby could have been Max's. I was too busy planning my wedding to Chris. The possibility didn't hit me until Dr. Young started talking about needing DNA samples."

"You know what we have to do, don't you?"

"What?"

"We've got to find Max."

"Does Lauren know where he is?"

"I doubt it, but that won't stop us; we'll hire a private detective and do whatever we have to to save Rowe."

"Thank you," Reese said, hugging Gillian close.

"For what?"

"For always being there for me."

"You'd do the same thing for me," Gillian said.

"I'd like to think so," Reese said, "but with my track record, I'm not so sure. I couldn't even do the right thing for my son."

"We are all a work in progress, no one is perfect, and that includes you, so lighten up and let's find Max."

Chapter 33

"Lauren, I refuse to believe that your mother, your prim, proper, Jack-and-Jill-founding-member mother, has been fucking Max for the last eight years! That is insane!" After Reese's confession of Rowe's paternity, Gillian thought that she'd heard it all. Max had officially slept with everyone in their group except her. And now *Mildred*? It was truly unbelievable.

"I understand. If I hadn't seen it with my own two eyes, I wouldn't believe it either." Lauren was still in shock. Without being aware of them, tears welled up in her eyes and spilled out down her cheek. The hurt was so deep that she was nearly numbed by it. It was difficult for her to comprehend the depth of her mother's betrayal.

"Lauren, are you okay?" Gillian could hear the grief in her friend's voice, even over the phone.

"I'm okay," she said unconvincingly. "It's just that everything I ever believed about my mom is a lie. I've always known that she was controlling and manipulative, but I also believed that she had my best interests at heart. I guess I was wrong there, too."

"You know that I know a little bit about manipulative mothers," Gillian said, trying to lighten the mood a little. "Early on I came to the conclusion that mothers are just people who happened to have birthed other people, and sometimes we put more weight on that title than is warranted since anyone is capable of being a manipulative, selfish—"

"Murderer?"

"Now, Lauren, just because she's a lying adulteress doesn't exactly make her a murderer."

Lauren repeated the poisonous pillow talk that she'd overheard between Mildred and Max. "I just don't know what to think. Clearly she hated Paulette not only for having the affair with Max, but for having his baby, and taking him from her, not to mention stealing the family's money, which by the way, was returned to the estate after Paulette's death. So, I say she wins the lottery for the person with the most motives for killing Paulette, especially if Paulette found out about her affair with Max. You know my cousin, she would definitely have held it over Mom's head, and I'm sure that Mom would have done anything to keep *that* secret buried, including burying Paulette."

"What about Brandon? He also had a good motive, and mobster connections. We know that your mom was in New York, and it's not as though she could flip through the yellow pages to find a killer."

"At this point I don't put anything past my mother."

"Do you think Max was in on it with her?" Gillian asked.

"It sure sounded that way to me. Speaking of Max, when I returned to the house today, Mom showed me the latest round of photos from online, then told me that she recognized a mole on the hip of the man in the photo. Max has one just like it, so she concluded that you and he were having an affair."

"Is it Max?"

"It looks like his body to me, but I'd trust my mother's judgment, since she obviously knows it a whole lot better than I do," Lauren smirked.

"So, why would she tell you that?"

"For one thing, at that point, she didn't know that I knew of their affair so there was no risk in her mind, but the main reason was to come between us. She's very jealous of our relationship, plus she was probably super-pissed at Max for betraying her yet again."

"I just thought of something," Gillian said, suddenly excited. "If it is Max in those pictures, that means I might be able to get to the bottom of this mess after all." Two birds, one stone, she thought. She could solve her problems and hopefully Reese's at the same time.

"That's a good point."

"There's something else I dread to tell you about Max," Gillian said hesitantly.

"Surely nothing could be worse than the fact that he's been fucking my mother."

Gillian cut to the chase and blurted it out. "He's the father of Reese's son, Rowe."

"What! You've gotta be kidding!"

"Afraid not. They had a drunken fling. She had a baby. And Chris footed the bill."

"I'll be damned," Lauren said, shaking her head.

"That's not all."

"Don't tell me you slept with him, too?" Lauren teased.

Gillian laughed. "That's one claim to fame that I'm happy not to have title to."

"What is it then?"

"Max may be Rowe's only chance at a bone marrow transplant, so we have to find Max to save the boy's life."

"Well, I heard my mom say that he's in Atlanta, so it can't be too hard. Let's do it."

"But, I thought you were leaving for Africa in the morning."

"It can wait. My life and everyone else's is in shambles and I need some closure before I leave. Hopefully by finding Max we can prove who killed Paulette, maybe figure out how and why and if he is sabotaging you, and hopefully save a life in the process."

"In that case, I'll fly to New York tomorrow, and we'll figure out where to go from here."

"Great. I've got a suite at the Gansevoort, so you can stay here with me."

"Cool. I'll call you when I land."

If it weren't for the fact that they were confronted with

a deceitful, adulterous mother, a scheming ex-husband, an unsolved murder, and the sabotage of Gillian's career, all with a child's life hanging in the balance, it might have been like the pajama parties they had in the good ole days.

Chapter 34

Tyrone pimped down Madison Avenue, confident that those who saw him were in total awe. And he was right, but not for the reasons he suspected. While his daisy yellow three-piece suit and matching full-length fur coat and hat may have been all the rage in Detroit in the seventies, in the Big Apple circa 2009 they were simply outrageous.

As he strolled along the avenue, with his coat swinging out behind him like Batman's cape, he flashed glimpses of the custom neon-orange silk lining for all to see. And see they did. Many stopped, stared, pointed, and gawked as though Tyrone were a newly discovered species fresh out of the Bronx Zoo.

He turned into Barneys to the dismay of the doormen and the concierge who were all too shocked by his appearance and his gall at having darkened their doors to say or do anything except watch as the yellow fur floated along behind him. They wanted to stop him, call security, or slam the doors shut, anything to prevent the tacky man from polluting the ultrachic confines of Barneys New York, but it was too late, he'd rung the call button for the elevator.

When he exited at the ninth floor and turned into Fred's, the watering hole for wealthy East Side executives, socialites, and fashionistas after a grueling day of shopping, all eyes turned to him. The room took a collective breath, then held it, waiting to witness the unfolding drama. Surely something was about to happen.

"I's here to meet Mr. Brandon Russell," he announced to the still-stunned hostess, as well as to the rest of the room.

"Ah-ah, yes," she stammered, desperate to compose herself. There was nothing in the training manual that told her what to do in the event someone so utterly tacky walked in during the height of lunchtime.

While she was still figuring it out, Tyrone caught sight of Brandon cowering like a freshly beaten dog in a corner, trying his best to hide behind a menu. "There he is. I'll seat myself," Tyrone said to the speechless hostess and took off in Brandon's direction with all eyes still tracking the blur of yellow.

Brandon looked as though he were trying to figure out how his two-hundred-pound frame might somehow fit beneath a two-top table.

"My man!" Tyrone exclaimed, reaching out for a high five.

Brandon grabbed his hand and pulled him down into the chair opposite him. "What the hell are you doing here?" he hissed, while his eyes darted furtively around.

"Whatchoo mean, what am I doing here? We gots serious business to discuss."

"Harold was supposed to be coming."

"Yeah, I know, but I thought this might be something best handled personally." He took a seat and reared back in it, then crossed his yellow and white, two-toned gaiters.

Brandon was furious; they'd agreed never to be seen in public together. He only met with Tyrone's attorney, and then only if absolutely necessary. There was no question that he never would have been taken seriously as a businessman if his association with the notorious drug kingpin from Mississippi were known. Worse, he'd probably be in jail given the feds' relentless investigation of him.

"You know we shouldn't be seen together?" Brandon hissed, glad he'd left his sunglasses in place. He was peering around the room and had already spotted Ron Pearlman at one table and Tracy Maitland at another, two very powerful and well-connected moguls in the city.

"What? Now that yo missus is a big celebrity you too big for me?" Tyrone bristled.

"That has nothing to do with it," Brandon lied.

"It has everything to do with it," Tyrone said, leaning forward menacingly. "Because of Gillian, the heat's been turned back up on this money laundering investigation, and me and the boys don't like it. We let things slide when you lost the damned flash drive, trusting you that the situation was buttoned up, but now this publicist chick is stirring up more trouble."

"Don't worry, I've got it under control," Brandon said.

"Somehow, it don't quite seem that way, but I suggest that you get it under control fast, or I'll handle things my way."

A chill ran down the length of Brandon's back. Being threatened by Tyrone had a tendency to do that to the bravest of men. Though his visual image was cartoonish, underneath the double-breasted, pastel three-piece suit there was nothing funny. He was a ruthless gangster, capable of whatever was necessary; in fact, there was a rumor that he'd had a hit put on his own son for freelancing drugs in his territory.

"I can assure you that won't be necessary," Brandon said. "I'll tie up all the loose ends."

"You do that," Tyrone said, squaring off the shoulders of his yellow mink, which he still wore, along with the hat.

Brandon was sure that his presence at Fred's was not a happenstance at all. Tyrone was sending the message that Brandon's past was right around the corner and could be in his face at a moment's notice. In other words, he could climb as far up the ladder as he wanted to, but his shady homeboys would always be just one rung away.

Chapter 35

Being the object of the story was so much more fun than merely reporting on it, Lydia mused. Now that *she* was the one being interviewed and *her* picture was running in article after article, even her good-for-nothing ex-fiancé had come slithering back and reproposed marriage. Everyone wanted to bask in the sunshine generated by a star, and that's what Lydia was now, a star, a media darling, and—who knew—maybe she'd even win a Pulitzer prize.

All of this glory was because of the little bitty zip drive that she'd accidentally found in Gillian's boudoir during a photo shoot.

While the stylist was busy steaming garments, Lydia suddenly remembered a funky pair of black suede boots that Gillian had that would be perfect with the outfit. Being the dutiful handholding publicist, she'd raced off to Gillian's closet to fetch them from the top shelf. When she pulled them out of the box, she heard something moving around in the toe of one. After removing the drive and a note, a puzzled expression settled on her face. Her first impulse was to simply give them both to Gillian, and the boots to the stylist, but something told her to hang on to them, so she stuffed both into her bra, put the boots back on the shelf, and then returned to the shoot as if nothing had happened.

Later that night, when she read Paulette's blackmail note, a shiver ran down her spine. By the time she'd opened the drive and seen its contents, she knew two things to be true: one, that Brandon *was* guilty of the money laundering charges that had been rumored, and two, most likely he was also guilty of murder. He had every possible motive. Anyone involved with gangsters certainly wouldn't be beyond killing a blackmailer to stay out of jail. Plus, Paulette's car was parked in his garage just before the accident.

Not sure what to do, she hid the evidence and decided to sleep on it. She knew that she should turn it over to the authorities, but also realized that if she did she'd be fired, losing her chance at the big times and most likely would be blackballed from the industry for snooping around a client's personal belongings. As fate would have it, the next day the article about the Italian Stallion broke and Imelda fired her anyway.

Lydia was devastated and thus saw no reason not to use the evidence to bring down the Russells and get the fame and fortune she deserved in the process.

Her tell-all book was now more than half done, and though filled with half-truths and barely veiled innuendo, it made for juicy reading. She, or her team of investigators, had interviewed over two dozen people, and the plan was to release the contents of the zip drive to authorities during a big press conference the day before the book was scheduled to come to a Borders or Barnes & Noble near you. Until then she'd kept the zip drive and the note locked in a metal box hidden under her bed.

Happy as a clam, she was ready to work on the manuscript for the next six hours, but first she needed a hit of cocaine to get the juices flowing. Fortunately her supplier, Randy, a dorky tech-type she'd met through a gay friend, was on his way over with enough blow to last her for at least a month.

When her doorbell rang, Lydia had it open before the last ring tone faded. She knew immediately that something was very wrong. Randy wore a terrified expression on his face; he looked like he'd seen a ghost. Before Lydia could ask him what was wrong, he was shoved in past her, and a guy the size of a sumo wrestler, and a second guy who looked like a wired crack addict, stormed in behind him.

"What the fuck—" she started, before the beefy stranger slammed the door shut and the smaller guy grabbed her in a flash and clasped a sweaty hand over her mouth. Randy stood there in total shock with his eyes bulging out of his head. He hadn't uttered a word since being accosted by the two thugs as soon as he got out of his car in front of Lydia's. They obviously knew exactly where he was headed and why.

Lydia twisted and turned trying to free herself. "We don't want to hurt you, but we will," the wiry guy hissed into her ear. She could smell his rancid, hot breath and wanted desperately to pull away. "We just want to have a conversation, that's all. We can do this nice and easy, or we can be a bit more persuasive," he threatened.

At that, Sumo Guy flashed a menacing-looking knife with a sharp serrated blade, which got her full attention.

"I'm gonna remove my hand, but if you make one noise that ain't an answer to our question, we'll introduce you and your punk-ass friend here to the tip of this blade."

When he took his hand away, Lydia was left gasping for air. Randy stood nearby shaking like a whore's ass; his eyes were the size of silver dollars.

Lydia tried gathering her racing thoughts to get a handle on what was going on and why. It seemed clear to her that this was not a drug heist; otherwise they would have simply taken what Randy had on him and not bothered involving another witness. With a feeling of dread she realized that she—not Randy—was the intended target. That's when she also realized the seriousness of what she'd done by stealing evidence from a gangster, then threatening to go public with it. Lydia suddenly felt very nauseous.

"I'll only ask once. I need you to give us what you took from a friend of ours, and I think you know what I'm talking about."

Lydia simply nodded. There was no use playing games with these guys, she was way out of her league.

"Take us to it," he demanded.

She led him into her bedroom, got on her knees, and pulled out the box. Without being asked Lydia put in the code and watched the door swing open. She reached in and felt both the note from Paulette and the flash drive, but on a whim she only pulled out the drive, leaving the note tucked safely inside. She reasoned they probably didn't know about the copy of the blackmail letter, which had been handwritten by Paulette, so why give it up when she might need it for leverage one day.

Cracky snatched the drive from her hand, kissed it, and announced, "It's been a pleasure doin' biznis with you." He stopped in the living room and turned back to her. "Oh, and by the way, that book you was writing? Forget about it, or we'll be paying you another visit, and that one won't be nearly as civil. Have a good day," he said, smiling to display a set of mustard-colored teeth that hadn't seen chloride in some time.

As he and Two Tons of Fun swaggered out her front door, along with her dreams of fame and fortune, Lydia was left deflated, with a shell-shocked Randy standing in a puddle of his own pee.

Chapter 36

"So, when do I get paid?" Charli demanded. It had been over a month since Max talked her into embarking on the sleazy smear campaign to destroy Gillian, and he still hadn't explained exactly how those raunchy photos—which she had never wanted to take—would translate into dollars in her pocket. Besides she'd been cooped up the whole time and was going stir crazy. With the photos all over the Internet and print magazines, Charli had to hide out for fear that she would be discovered now that she was styled exactly like her famous twin sister.

"Don't worry about it," Max said. "I'll contact Gillian's publicist today and I'm sure that Brandon will pay a pretty penny to keep more pictures or the video from cropping up."

"But isn't that illegal?" Charli was beginning to have serious second thoughts about the whole thing. She had gone along with the harebrained scheme in a misguided attempt to get back at her estranged mother and sister, but never expected her own face and body to be plastered on Internet sites around the globe. What had she been thinking?

The idea of a stripper/whore suddenly growing a conscience was ridiculous to Max. "So is prostitution," he snapped.

The comment stung sharply. She'd made the fatal mistake of believing that Max could care for anyone except himself. "I am *not* a prostitute!" Charli shouted.

"What else do you call someone who sells their body for money?"

She had to struggle to hold back her tears. "I'm out of here," she said.

Charli should have known that Max was too good to be true. While he looked smooth and sophisticated on the outside, she was quickly learning that he was as slimy as they came. In many ways he was much worse than Flash ever was; at least with Flash you knew up front what you were dealing with, but with Max, his movie-star good looks and veneer of charm and elegance were dangerously deceiving.

Realizing that he might have gone too far, Max grabbed her gently, "Charli, I'm sorry. I shouldn't have said that. I know that you were only a dancer and not a prostitute. I'm just under a lot of pressure and I took it out on you. I'm deeply sorry." He still needed Charli to wrap up his business with Brandon and Gillian.

"I'm tired of this. I can't do it anymore."

"One more day, that's all." Max gave her his most charming partial smile, and then hugged her close to his chest. If he had to he'd give her what most women wanted. A little sex always did the trick.

"You promise?"

"I promise," he said. "I'll tell you what. I've got to run a few errands, so why don't I pick up dinner from Kozmos and a bottle of your favorite wine and we'll have a nice relaxed evening?"

"Okay." She was too exhausted and drained to do anything but go along with his suggestion. Besides, she didn't exactly have a lot of choices or a plan of her own.

Feeling comfortable that he'd regained control of the situation, Max grabbed his coat and headed out the door.

Two minutes later the doorbell rang. Thinking that he must have left his house key and returned to retrieve it, Charli trudged to the door and opened it right away.

On the other side stood her mirror image, wearing the identical mouth-agape, wide-eyed expression, staring right back at her.

Chapter 37

Gillian was frozen solid in shock, not comprehending how someone who looked exactly like her could be standing on the other side of the door staring right back at her. "Oh, my God," she whispered. "This can't be." She slowly began to understand how the pictures that weren't her and also weren't doctored could be so real.

Neither Charli nor Gillian moved a muscle for fear of shattering the mirror image that bewildered them both.

Lauren, who stood also stunned at Gillian's side, looked from one twin to the other trying to make sense out of the strange tableau before her eyes. As far as she'd ever known, Gillian was—and always had been—an only child. Even though Lauren had a brother who'd long ago escaped the clutches of their controlling and manipulative mother, she'd always felt like an only child herself, which was part of the reason that she and Gillian had adopted each other as sisters.

"Who are you?" Lauren asked, breaking their uneasy standoff.

"I'm Charli." The words formed themselves and left her mouth, while Charli's eyes never left Gillian's. There was a magical connection, which she felt instantly, and intuitively she realized why she'd never felt complete before this moment. All of those empty years, feeling as if she didn't belong had nothing to do with Miner, Missouri, or her adoptive parents, but everything to do with the woman standing in front of her. Her other half.

"Charli, I'm Lauren." Lauren extended her hand, hoping to ease both women back down to reality, and do so before Max showed up. "Do you mind if we come in?"

A private detective Lauren hired had led them to Atlanta and Charli's condo, which Max had essentially moved into. They flew in that afternoon, and immediately camped out in front. When they saw Max leave, they decided to talk to whoever this Charli person was before confronting Max. They didn't know if Charli was male or female and certainly had no idea that the owner would be Gillian's identical twin.

Charli stepped aside so that Gillian and Lauren could enter. Once they were all seated around a coffee table, Charli hid her face and whimpered, "I'm *so* sorry." The tears she'd been holding back began to fall freely. Some fell from relief at having found something that she hadn't even realized was lost, and others fell out of shame at how it had all come about. "I didn't want to do the pictures. I'm so sorry," she repeated.

Gillian's tears began to fall also. Charli's words were not even necessary; somehow Gillian could feel her pain and emotions, as clearly as if they were her own. "It's okay" was all she said. All of the anger that had built up at those responsible for the awful photos disappeared. Nothing, including an Oscar, was as real for her as this moment.

"It's really okay," she repeated.

Those were the words Charli had needed to hear her entire life. That it was okay. That *she* would be okay. For no reason other than the fact that they were together now, she believed it. The smoldering sense of doom that had hung over Charli her entire life already felt lighter. She had none of the anger at her sister that Max had been planting in her heart.

Lauren hated to break up the magical moment, but she realized that Max could return at any moment and they needed to have a plan by then. "Where is Max?" she asked.

"He went out to run an errand and pick up dinner. He should be gone at least a couple of hours."

"Charli, I don't know how well you know him, but he's my ex-husband, and trust me, he is a very conniving and possibly even dangerous man."

Charli shook her head slowly. "I'm beginning to see that. I don't know how I could have been so stupid."

"He's fooled a lot of people for a long time, including me."

"You said 'dangerous.' What do you mean?" Charli asked.

"He may have had something to do with the murder of

my cousin, Paulette, whom he was also having an affair with."

A shiver ran down Charli's spine. She'd been foolish enough to believe that the suave and sophisticated Max cared so much about her that he would save her from Flash and his sleazy world, but she was now realizing that she hopped out of the frying pan right into a blazing fire. "I only recently met him—two months ago." She lowered her head in shame. "I was at my lowest point. My mother had just passed, and I'd just found out that I was adopted."

She explained some parts of her childhood and how she'd ended up in the Atlanta strip joint where Max had found her.

Gillian's heart was broken over the tragedy that her sister's life had been. The fact that Charli had posed for pornographic pictures to ruin her own life didn't matter. She'd learned from Paulette that good people sometimes did bad things because of their pasts. "I'm so sorry that you had to go through that," she said, reaching over to embrace her twin. They held on to each other as though their lives were inextricably tied to the other.

Watching the sisters bond after so much time, tragedy, and disappointment, Lauren felt a wave of sadness that she and Paulette had never gotten to that point. But the least she could do for her cousin was to get to the bottom of who killed her.

"Ladies, I hate to break up the family reunion, but we've got some loose ends to tie up."

"Yeah, named Maximillian Neuman, the Third," Gillian said.

"I'm in," Charli said, "In fact, I'd like to tie *him* up." She smiled for the first time in months. It felt good to be a part of a team, and most importantly to have found family.

Chapter 38

Heading into the Gansevoort, Lauren walked past Pastis, the chic French bistro in New York's Meat-packing District, where she, Reese, Gillian, and Paulette's lives forever became intertwined.

It was eight years ago, and Lauren had just graduated from Harvard, when she met Paulette for lunch there to tell her the exciting news that she was moving to New York to attend Columbia Law School. It was not the news that Paulette wanted to hear. She'd built About Time Publicity in New York and made a name for herself separate and apart from her snotty relatives and wasn't looking forward to sharing the spotlight with her drop-dead gorgeous and rich cousin.

Afterward, while they were walking up Ninth Avenue, they ran into Reese, who invited Lauren to a party that she and Paulette were attending and that Paulette had conveniently forgotten to mention to Lauren when asked about hanging out later. Gillian, who was Reese's roommate at the time, also joined them, and from then on the mismatched foursome had been joined at the hip in an intense love-and-sometimes-hate relationship.

Those days seemed both like yesterday and over a century ago. Lauren felt Paulette's presence as she walked down memory lane, ending up back at her hotel. It was a comforting presence, since she'd long since forgiven Paulette for having that disastrous affair with her husband, and now, more than ever, realized that Max was quite capable of manipulating Paulette into it for his own selfish gain.

Gideon had been a godsend after Paulette's tragic death and her dramatic break up with Max. He was the most grounded, caring, and introspective person she'd ever met. Over the last three years they had traveled the world together documenting diverse cultures through photography for his gallery in Williamsburg as well as for publications such as *National Geographic*. It was a bohemian existence that was literally worlds away from the country club/Jack-and-Jill life that Mildred had mapped out for Lauren.

Thinking about her mother was a painful exercise that Lauren tried to avoid, especially over the last week, after catching her and Max en flagrante. Though Mildred didn't realize it, Lauren had kept in contact with her father over the years, having him call her whenever he could do so in privacy. The hardest decision she'd made was to tell him about her mother and Max's sordid affair, as well as their possible complicity in Paulette's death.

Nathan was understandably shocked. Though he knew

his wife well and realized that she was both selfish and manipulative, he would never have imagined that she would stoop to having an affair with her own son-in-law or murdering her own niece. The very next day he moved out of the family's estate and into an apartment in Manhattan.

Lauren's family was now permanently shattered; leaving a gaping hole in her heart that ached much more than she cared to admit.

"Hey, sweetie," Lauren said when Gideon picked up the phone. He was in Niger photographing the Touareg tribe. It was early evening there, so Lauren figured he would be done shooting for the day.

"How's my girl?" he asked. He'd checked on her every day since she told him about her mother and Max.

She could hear the smile in his voice, which made her ache to see it in person. "I've been better," she answered.

"I wish I were there to hold you."

"I could really use a big hug right now."

A knock at her hotel room door caused Lauren to frown, since she'd not ordered room service, nor was she expecting anyone. "Just a minute," she said, putting the call on hold.

She went to the door and looked cautiously through the peephole. There stood Gideon wearing a big beautiful smile.

"What are you doing here?!" she asked, leaping into his arms and wrapping hers around his neck.

"You said you could use a hug, so here I am."

"I can't believe you're really here." She'd missed him badly, even more so after the explosion with her mom.

"You know there's no way I'd let you go through this alone, especially knowing how unpredictable and possibly dangerous Max is."

"You really didn't have to travel here all the way from Africa," she said, "but I'm so glad you did." She hadn't realized just how badly she needed him.

"I'm glad I did, too," he said.

Once inside the suite, he led her to the sofa where he held her close. Tears trekked silently down her face while he kissed them away, helping to ease some of the hurt. She'd never felt more loved, safe, and secure.

Chapter 39

Working through a sleazy attorney, Max reached out to CoAnne Wilshire to negotiate a settlement with Brandon and Gillian. If they wired two hundred and fifty thousand dollars into a numbered bank account, he promised the smear campaign would stop. He also warned them that the video and the next round of photos would be even more damaging than anything previously seen by the public.

In their final photo shoot, a naked and dazed-appearing Charli was snorting what looked to be coke from a glass tray covered in drug paraphernalia and blunts. It was vintage Amy Winehouse. While sex sells, including movie tickets, drugs—especially done by a glamorous female movie star— were a deal breaker in Hollywood. Gillian's Oscar bid—if not her career—would be dead once and for all if those photos ever hit the Internet.

To help Brandon come to the right decision about whether to part with a chunk of his cash, Max sent him a sample shot. The ploy worked like a charm; he'd just gotten word from CoAnne that Brandon had agreed to wire the funds first thing in the morning. Game. Set. Match. It was time to party!

"Let's toast to our success!" he said, handing Charli another glass from their second bottle of Veuve Clicquot.

"Finally!" Charli said, smiling broadly. "I was beginning to think all those photos and shit were for nothing."

"You should know I'd never let you down, baby," he said, leaning over to kiss her, marveling at how well he'd transformed her into her glamorous twin.

"I'll never doubt you again," she said, getting up to give him a full view of her sexy attire. She wore a short lace teddy designed to bring boys and men to their knees.

"You'd better not or I might have to spank you," he said, patting her behind possessively.

"So, what's next?" She sat on his lap and gazed into his eyes.

The four glasses of Champagne, the joint he'd smoked, and the promise of money were making Max both relaxed and happy. "What do you want?" he asked, rubbing her back.

"I like this Bonnie and Clyde thing we pulled off, so I think we should set up our next heist." She gave him a devilish look.

"Are you sure you're up to that? You were a little queasy on this one," Max quizzed.

"That's because it was my first time with you, but now

that I see you know what you're doing, I'm down. But I do have a confession to make."

"What is it?"

"It's about my past," she said in a very serious tone. "Now that I'm your Bonnie, I feel like you have to know everything. The good, the bad, and the ugly."

"Go on," he prompted, anxious to hear just how low Charli would go.

"A couple of years ago, I was involved with a guy who was a drug dealer. I went with him on an exchange that got ugly. While I was hiding in an alleyway, the buyer pulled a gun and tried to rob Julio. I came out, pulled the gun that Julio had given me, and shot him. He died."

"Wow, okay," Max said, shaking his head. Though he knew that she had been a stripper and probably a prostitute, he hadn't realized that his little Charli was a real-life Bonnie. She may be just the kind of chick he needed, at least for now.

"I felt bad, but I did what I had to do," she said, in her toughest street posturing.

"There's nothing wrong with that," Max said, admiringly.

"Are you sure you want me around?"

Oh, he definitely wanted her around. Someone disposable and willing to do anything could certainly come in handy during the course of a scam. "Of course I do, baby."

"Are you sure?" She looked teary, as though worried about whether or not he would accept her.

"Absolutely. Hey, I'm no innocent myself," he said.

She poured him another glass of Champagne. "But I know a softy like you has never killed anyone," she said, teasing him. "I don't think you'd have the balls for it," she challenged.

"Don't be so sure," he answered. There was no way that he'd let her think that she was tougher than he was. That was no way to start a Bonnie and Clyde relationship. Clyde always had to be on top.

A gleam of excitement lit up her eyes as she squirmed in his lap, giving him an instant hard on. This was one of the tricks Charli had learned in the strip clubs. "Do tell, this is making me very hot," she purred into his ear.

"No, I'd better not," he said, though his eyes were rapidly glazing over in lust.

She stopped her grinding and took a stern tone. "I told you about me, so you have to tell me about you. It's only fair. Plus you know I'd never tell anyone. If I did you'd tell on me, and I'm not trying to go back to jail."

Hmm, so she'd been to jail, Max thought. Charli was proving to be a regular little hood rat.

She grabbed his dick in her hand and began massaging it slowly. "So tell me," she crooned. "I am getting soooo wet."

And he was getting soooo hard. "Let's just say that me and a friend had to take care of someone who was blackmailing us." He left out the full list of motives that he and Mildred shared. It was bad enough that Paulette was having his baby, but when she found out that he and Mildred were having an affair, she threatened to expose them both unless he left Lauren and married her, and Mildred forked over half a million in cash.

"So, how'd you do it?" she purred in his ear, while still stroking his dick.

"We sent her boy Joe out to L.A. to cut her brake line, sent that bitch right over into the canyons around Mulholland Drive. Trust me, she got just what she deserved."

"Who is we?" Charli pouted. "You got another Bonnie?"

"Not anymore, baby," he moaned. Lately, Charli had been holding back the sex, so he couldn't wait to get down to business now that they were both all steamed up. "Miss Mildred is yesterday's news."

"You sure I don't have anything to worry about?" She gave him the puppy dog eyes.

"From that old skank? Not at all, baby. It's you and me now. Go ahead and give me one of your famous stripteases."

She stood up and he leaned back on the sofa and took out his dick, stroking it in his hand as he prepared for his appetizer, knowing that his entree would be well worth the wait.

Charli began to slowly move her hips in a seductive grind. Her hands glazed over her breasts before sliding down between her cleavage. When she removed them, she also removed a very small listening device, which she held up and dangled in front of Max's lust-filled eyes.

"What is that?" he asked.

"Your one-way ticket to jail," she answered. The seduction was gone from her voice, replaced by pure venom.

He slowly began to understand that he'd been set up to

confess. Max jumped from the sofa, reaching for the device, but was too slow.

Before he got to her, the door to the condo burst open and two men dressed in suits appeared with guns drawn. "Put your hands in the air, where I can see them," one man's voice boomed.

"You bitch!" he hissed to Charli. Then he remembered his leverage. "Officer this is a big mistake. You can't believe anything she says. She is a prostitute who killed a man and has even been to jail. Her name is Charli Kemble."

"I don't think so," another voice said. Max turned toward the door and there stood another Charli.

"What the fuck?" Now he was totally confused.

"I'm Charli," the twin in the door said.

"And I'm Gillian," the twin who he'd thought was Charli, said.

"And you're fucked," Lauren said, entering the condo with Gideon at her side. She turned to Gillian and said, "Congrats on another award-winning performance." She, Charli, and Gillian all gave each other high fives, while Max stood by dazed and confused.

Chapter 40

Gillian should have been elated after solving the elusive three-year-old question of who killed Paulette, and also putting to rest the smear campaign designed to ruin her Oscar nomination and career, and finding Rowe's father. But her satisfaction was dampened by the prospects of two conversations that were long overdue. It was time for her and Brandon to both remove their rose-colored glasses and talk honestly and truthfully with each other. Then she'd have to have a "coming to Jesus" with Imelda. This time her mom had finally gone too far with the family secrets, and Gillian was over it.

She dropped her coat and handbag on the foyer table and entered the study where she knew Brandon would be taking his predinner cocktail. She figured she might as well get it over with.

Just as she thought, he was at his desk reviewing a contract. "Hi," she said.

He looked up at Gillian, and hesitated slightly before

standing up to greet her. He seemed to know what was coming, and wasn't looking forward to it. "How are you?" he asked.

"I'm okay."

"Can I get something for you?" He gestured to the nearby wet bar.

Though she'd love to have a glass of wine to take the edge off, she thought better of it. This was a conversation that was best had stone cold sober. "No, thanks," she said, before taking a seat.

Brandon poured himself a double vodka gimlet, before joining her on the sofa. He crossed his ankle atop his knee. "Welcome home, baby. From all accounts it sounds as if everything worked out perfectly down in Atlanta," he said. Brandon and CoAnne had coordinated the acceptance of Max's bribe to help set up the sting operation in conjunction with Lauren, Gillian, Charli, and the police in both Los Angeles and Atlanta.

"I suppose you could say that. I'm just glad it's all over." At least most of it was; there were still some loose ends to tie up before the arrests would be announced to the public. Meanwhile they had all been sworn to secrecy.

"Great job getting Max to confess to Paulette's murder. At least now you know I didn't kill her," he said in a weak attempt at sarcasm. Once he found out that Gillian had had the missing flash drive at one point, and the rumors that he killed Paulette resurfaced with news of the tell-all book, he knew that Gillian had to have suspected him, especially after she realized that he lied to her about the laundered money.

"I have a confession." Gillian decided to lay all of her chips on the table and let them fall where they may. "After Paulette was killed, and I went to New York with Reese, I came home with a blackmail note that Paulette had written to you and the flash drive proving you laundered the drug money. I didn't know what to do. I should have told you I had the drive and I was planning to, until I read the note and wondered whether or not you may have killed Paulette. I'm sorry for doubting you without even bothering to ask you."

"A blackmail note? You had a copy of that?" He hadn't realized that Paulette left a copy behind, since it wasn't among the things Tyrone's thugs got from Lydia.

Gillian was surprised that he didn't react to her finding the drive, only the letter. "Do *you* have the drive?" she asked. When she and Lauren discovered it was missing, they had turned the house upside down trying to find it. They figured that either Max or Imelda had it, since no one else had much access to the house.

"Not exactly. Lydia stole it from you and was planning to use the information in her book."

"I can't believe that Lydia would do that. So, where is it now?" she asked.

"Let's just say that the stolen property was stolen once again." Tyrone sent word to Brandon through his attorney that the package was wrapped up. He hadn't asked for any details, nor were any offered.

"How are you going to handle these drug people? You can't live your life with them hovering in the background."

"I know. I've got a plan to sort it all out," he promised.

He'd avoided confronting them in the past, but he now realized that in order to have control of his own future, he'd have to deal with them, one way or the other. "I didn't mean to get you wrapped up in all of this, I'm really sorry."

He decided to try to explain to his wife how he'd ended up where he was. "When I was much younger, trying to make my first CD out of my mother's basement in Mississippi, I borrowed money from the only place people like us could, since the banks wouldn't loan money to blacks back then, the local drug dealer. It wasn't a lot of money, but he's held it over my head since then, using threats and intimidation. I did not use their money to build Sound Entertainment, unless you count a three-hundred-dollar loan, which was paid back, but I was forced to launder their money as my and their business thrived. The more I agreed to do to keep quiet what I'd done already, the more they asked me to do. It just never stopped. I can't tell you how often I've regretted that decision. I've tried to be clean ever since, but the streets still cling to me, regardless of how far and fast I run. I just didn't want you to know about it." He hung his head in shame. As bad as he felt, he also felt lighter for having unburdened himself of a forty-year-old secret.

"It's okay, Brandon. We all make mistakes. *None* of us is perfect," Gillian said. "I knew about the double books, and married you anyway, doubts and all."

"Why?"

"I shouldn't have, but I guess I was more interested in getting what I wanted than in the truth. In that respect, I'm certainly no saint."

Brandon set his drink on the side table. "I just wish I hadn't lied to you about what was on the flash drive, then you probably wouldn't have doubted me about Paulette. I just wanted to be perfect for you and give you everything you deserved and wanted."

"If I haven't learned anything else from all of this, I've learned there is no such thing as perfection."

"I'm certainly not." Brandon took a sip of his drink, closed his eyes, and made a decision. "While I'm at it, I have another apology to make."

"What is it?"

"I never should have doubted that it wasn't you in those pictures, especially after you told me that it wasn't."

"Who knew that I had an identical twin sister?"

"But I do know you, and I should have believed you instead of letting jealousy, pride, and anger get in the way."

Gillian reached over and touched his hand. "We've both made a lot of mistakes."

"So where do we go from here?" Brandon asked. "You know I love you with all my heart," he pleaded. "And that will never change."

"I really don't know," Gillian said. "I think this time we should take it slow and think about everything before making any decisions." Though she'd grown to love Brandon, their foundation was built on lies and deception, and she wasn't sure that their love was enough to sustain them.

"That's fair."

"I'll move into the guesthouse until we figure it out," Gillian offered.

"I won't have that. Besides, you're not leaving me in this house with your mother," he joked. "Not to mention, where will Charli live?" He hadn't met his new sister-in-law yet, but was looking forward to having another version of Gillian in his life.

"I've asked her to come out to L.A. She's wrapping up some business in Atlanta right now and should be here tomorrow sometime." Gillian couldn't hide her excitement at the thought of having her sister by her side.

"In that case, it's all settled," Brandon announced. "The three of you can stay in the main house, and I'll move into the guesthouse. We can decide what to do about us after the Oscars."

"Thank you, Brandon."

"No, thank you. I just want another chance to get things right between us."

They both stood up and hugged each other, not knowing if this was the beginning of the end or the start of a new beginning.

Chapter 41

Two Louis Vuitton steamer trunks lay open on the floor of Mildred's bedroom, as she and James scurried about packing for her hastily arranged trip abroad. She wasn't sure how long she'd be gone, but given everything, this felt like a good time to leave for a month or so.

Since Nathan left, the gossips around New York had started stirring the pot, adding a little extra spice here and there, with the rumor that she was having an affair, along with the speculation that it had something to do with the tell-all book that was supposed to be written about her niece's death. Even though Mildred would have been ready to dish the dirt right along with them had it been anyone else, she still resented them for piling it on.

Well, she'd fix those nosy bitches; Mildred was going to leave the country until well after all this nonsense had died down. Soon enough people would be presented with another delicious new scandal to focus on. Hopefully, one not involving her.

She could kill Lauren for telling Nathan about Max. So what she caught them having an affair? It wasn't as if Lauren were still married to the man. Besides she didn't appreciate him when she had him, which was why he was still crawling into Mildred's bed at every opportunity, not to mention that hussy Paulette's, who truly got what she deserved. It was one thing for her to steal Mildred's money—she let her slide with that—and worse that she was having an affair with her daughter's husband and planning to have his baby—Mildred let her slide with that one, too—but for the gross heifer to try to take her man? The bitch had to pay for that one.

Mildred had no idea that Paulette was on to them until the no-class hussy had the nerve to stop by the house demanding a half a million dollars and that Max leave Lauren (and Mildred) and marry her, or else she would spill the beans. That was her fatal mistake. Mildred and Max agreed that under no circumstances could they allow either of those scenarios to unfold.

When Lauren told her mother that she, Reese, and Paulette were having a baby shower at Gillian and Brandon's house in the hills surrounding L.A., they decided that this was the perfect opportunity to get rid of Paulette once and for all. The only thing they needed was someone to cut the brake line, knowing that as soon as she started down the hill, it would be a very bumpy ride. So Mildred called Joe, a gardener who'd once worked for her until she discovered that he had a criminal record, a fact which now came in very handy. For fifty thousand dollars and two nights at a hotel in

L.A. with room service thrown in, he'd gladly followed Paulette up to Brandon's house, parked down the street, and then snuck around the property to the garage where all the cars were parked. Mildred hadn't realized that Reese would be riding with Paulette, and when she learned that Reese had been critically injured, she merely chalked it up to collateral damage.

"Madam, would you like for me to pack summer clothes as well?" James asked. James had no idea what was going on, except that Master Reynolds stormed out with a few suitcases days ago, and now the Madam had him packing steamer trunks full of clothes though she hadn't yet said where she was going.

"A bit of everything. I'll be gone awhile." She had a 7:30 p.m. reservation on Virgin Atlantic into Paris de Gaulle. She'd always enjoyed the City of Lights, and loved staying at the Plaza Athenee, and of course, the shopping was world class.

"Will Master Reynolds be joining you, Madam?"

"Do you see him, James?" Mildred snapped. As much as Mildred dreaded being caught in her affair, fear of losing her marriage wasn't the biggest reason, her reputation was. In many ways it was wildly liberating to finally be free of Nathan, who was such a drag. Sure, their families were the perfect match for each other, but boy what a stick in the mud! Once she'd gotten a taste of Max, she could barely stand for the old codger to look at her, let alone come waving his dried-up noodle her way.

Thinking of Max gave her a splendid idea. Maybe she

should invite him along on her little escapade. It would be perfect! No one knew them in Paris, so they could hang out together somewhere other than in a locked bedroom, like young lovers enjoying sunsets and small quaint cafés.

As pissed off as she was at Max for having an affair with that no good slut Gillian, her hormones shooed her anger away. After all, she was married, so she couldn't really expect him to be celibate. But now that she'd also decided to divorce Nathan, she was positive that he would be faithful to her. She'd be Mrs. Maximillian Neuman III. Maybe they'd even live overseas where no one would know them.

Thrilled at the idea, she snatched up the phone to call his cell. She got no answer. She then dialed his condo in Buckhead, Atlanta. Still no answer, but she did leave a message. Desperate now to reach him, she picked up her Black-Berry and sent an e-mail and a text message. It read: On way to Paris. Call ASAP. Wld luv 4 u to join me for a long, romantic rendezvous!

She was just starting to pack her toiletries when the doorbell rang. While she was deciding between Annick Goutal's Les Nuits d'Hadrien or Eau d'Hadrien, James appeared in the doorway wearing the most ridiculously sheepish expression.

"What is it, James? Can't you see that I'm packing?" He was such an idiot sometimes. She often wondered why she'd kept him all these years, but she knew the answer. James, and before him, his father, and his father's father, had always worked for the Baines family.

"Madam, there are some men here to speak to you."

"What men? Who could possibly be dropping by without an appointment? You know I don't welcome uninvited guests." She continued to pack, dismissing James, and the men.

"Madam?"

"What are you doing still standing there?"

"It's the police," he nearly whispered.

This got her attention. "Did they say what they wanted?"

"Only to speak with you."

"What about, James?" she demanded. Of course they wanted to speak to her, that much was obvious, but what about? That was the key question.

"They wouldn't tell me," James answered, though truthfully, he didn't have the courage to even think about questioning the police. Once they flashed their badges, he scurried away to find Mildred quicker than a sand crab on the beach.

"I'll be right down," she said to the useless man. What good was a butler if he couldn't even screen unwanted visitors, regardless if they were the police.

He stood frozen in place, as though waiting to walk out tucked behind Mildred's skirts. "Go, please, go. Tell them I'll be right down." She needed to think and couldn't possibly do so with James looking at her like a scared puppy dog. He eventually scampered away.

What could they possibly want? Mildred wondered, as she began pacing back and forth, the shops along the

Champs-Elysées long forgotten. And where was Max? Did one thing have something to do with the other? Beads of sweat suddenly materialized on her brow. She'd never seriously considered that she could ever be arrested. It just seemed like an impossibility that Mildred Baines-Reynolds could ever be accused of something so foul as murder. After all, she was a well-respected member of society.

But what if they did arrest her? What if her neighbors and Page Six were already at the end of the driveway waiting to get a shot of the perp walking to the back of the police car? Maybe Max turned on her and that's why she couldn't reach him.

Panic overtook Mildred as her thoughts raced along. She couldn't bear the thought of being arrested. Just the idea of a mug shot was frightening enough. Maybe she should put on some lipstick just in case. She couldn't decide whether to freshen her makeup or jump out the window. Fortunately, she didn't have to.

"Mrs. Baines-Reynolds?" A burly detective asked as he appeared in her doorway.

"I tried to stop them, Madam, but they insisted."

"That's okay, James," Mildred said in her strongest high-society voice.

"I'm Detective Henderson, and this is my partner, Detective Jones." While his partner spoke, Detective Jones, a middle-aged white man with a thin comb-over, scanned the room, not missing a speck.

"Please, have a seat." She gestured to the sitting area in her expansive master suite. "Sorry to keep you waiting."

"You planning a trip?" Detective Henderson asked, while his partner roamed around, taking it all in.

"Heading to Paris for a little shopping," Mildred answered. Her composure had instinctively turned to steel.

"Going alone?"

"In fact, I am."

"Where is your husband?"

His tone was now quite offensive. There was no way that Mildred Baines-Reynolds would be treated so commonly in her own home. "Officer, I don't mean to be rude, but could you tell me what this is about?"

"Absolutely," Officer Henderson said, leaning forward. "It's about your niece's murder."

"What does that have to do with me?" she asked, pulling a cigarette from Nathan's ebony box that sat on the cocktail table. She hadn't smoked in ten years, but the urge for nicotine was overwhelming. Actually, what she really wanted was a nice stiff drink, but James, of course, was nowhere to be found.

"Quite a bit, it seems," Detective Jones intoned from across the room.

"I spoke with detectives after Paulette's death and told them everything that I knew."

"Except for one small detail," Detective Jones rebutted. "That you were both sleeping with the same man, your daughter's husband."

He delivered his uppercut in one smooth stroke, sending Mildred reeling. How the fuck did they find that out, she wondered. Surely Lauren wouldn't tell them, even though she had told Nathan. Mildred braced herself and forged ahead. "That had nothing whatsoever to do with Paulette's murder."

"Except for when she threatened to expose it."

"I did not kill Paulette," she insisted, injecting defiance into her voice, all the while puffing away on her cigarette, trying but failing to channel Marlene Dietrich.

"Oh, so Max did it?" Detective Henderson asked.

"I didn't say that."

"But according to him you were involved in the plot to kill your niece."

A bolt of shock ran through Mildred. Her hand shook in terror. Would Max really have thrown her under the bus?

"I don't know what you're talking about."

"Maybe you need a little reminder," Detective Jones said before whipping a tape recorder from his pocket. He pressed play and Max's voice filled the room:

> "Let's just say that me and a friend had to take care of someone who was blackmailing us."
>
> "So how'd you do it?" a female voice asked.
>
> "We sent her boy Joe out to L.A. to cut her brake line, sent that bitch right over into the canyons around Mulholland Drive. Trust me, she got just what she deserved."
>
> "Who is we?" The woman asked. "You got another Bonnie?"
>
> "Not anymore, baby," he moaned. "Miss Mildred is yesterday's news."

"You sure I don't have anything to worry about?"

"From that old skank? Not at all, baby. It's you and me now. Go ahead and give me one of your famous stripteases."

By the time the tape ended, Mildred had aged twenty years. Not only did she have frightening visions of stripes that weren't from the fall collections, she also felt like an old fool for ever believing in Max. In fact, what hurt the most was that he'd called her "an old skank."

Mildred put the cigarette out and said, "I need to speak to my attorney."

Chapter 42

Imelda tiptoed around Gillian and Brandon's house like a mouse navigating a house full of hungry cats. Now was the time for her to not be seen *or* heard, both concepts that heretofore were foreign to Imelda, who could always be counted on to be the most visible woman in any room.

But times were a changing. After firing Lydia, which sparked the whole revenge tell-all book saga, followed by the embarrassing revelation about Gillian's supposedly dead father and the ensuing dustup with Gillian, Imelda was just happy to have a handcrafted, multimillion-dollar roof over her head.

Even more troubling was the building discord between Gillian and Brandon. He seemed to believe that the nude shots of Gillian being circulated were real, and she seemed disinterested in convincing him otherwise. Imelda didn't know whether the photos were of her daughter or not, and she really didn't care—after all, everybody made mistakes, she'd certainly made enough of her own—she only prayed that Gillian had enough sense to hang on to Brandon for both of their sakes.

As an Oscar-nominated actress, Gillian (and thus Imelda) wouldn't be collecting food stamps, but it would be many long years before they could afford the lavish lifestyle that Brandon handed them on a silver platter. And Imelda was much too comfortable in her richly appointed wing of the estate, with an on-call butler, a chauffeur-driven fleet of luxury cars, and no bills at all, to *ever* want to leave. Hell, if she could fuck and marry Brandon herself she would; however, she'd finally come to the very harsh realization that her own legendary gold-digging days were well over. No amount of Botox, breast jobs, or designer wardrobes would enable her to compete with women ten, twenty, and thirty years younger than she. Her looks had finally betrayed her for good.

Now she only hoped that no more of those scandalous photos came out and that Gillian would win that Oscar. She also prayed that Gillian would go ahead and have a baby, which would ensure them at least another eighteen years of checks.

There was a knock at the door to her suite, startling Imelda since no one, except the cleaning woman, ever came to the west wing. "Who is it?"

"It's me, Mom."

"Oh, come on in, honey."

Gillian walked in and plopped down on her mother's chaise longue.

"Is everything okay?" Imelda asked.

Gillian ignored the question. "I want you to be completely honest with me. Is there something else that you need to tell me about my family?" she asked.

Imelda thought hard, but couldn't think of anything important. "No, why do you ask?"

"The pictures Mom. How do you think they were done?" Gillian wanted desperately for her mother to confess that she'd given away one of her babies, thinking that honesty—however late—would somehow make it a little better.

"Sweetie, I have no idea. I mean, they must have used that computer stuff on them, unless they really are you. After all, we all make mistakes."

Gillian was furious and struggled to keep the anger from her voice. "I told you that it wasn't me."

"If it is, you can tell me. I won't tell anybody."

"Just like you didn't tell anybody about your second child?" There, she'd said it.

"What are you talking about?" Imelda looked genuinely bewildered.

At that moment, Gillian hated her mother. What nerve. For her to look Gillian in her eyes and boldly deny the existence of a child that she gave birth to was unconscionable!

"How could you do that? How could you give away one of your own babies?" Gillian screamed. "How did you choose which of us to give away? Was it as simple as a coin toss?"

Imelda looked dumbfounded. The pressure must finally

be getting to Gillian, she thought. "I have no idea what you're talking about," she insisted.

"Or do you mean, who?" Charli said, entering the suite. She stood next to her sister looking like a duplicate.

Imelda sat there with her mouth agape, and her eyes wide in open-faced astonishment. "I-I-I don't understand," was all that she could manage to say. "What's going on?" she asked, looking from one to the other. Shock was written all over her face.

"It's simple, Mom. You obviously couldn't be burdened with *two* babies and just decided to leave one of us behind. You took my sister from me, and me from her," Gillian charged.

"That's not true!" Imelda insisted, snapping out of her shock.

The Oscar should simply go straight to her mother, Gillian thought. She'd never seen a more convincing performance in her life, but the proof stood before them both.

"Stop lying, Mom. Meet your other daughter, Charli," Gillian spat.

Imelda was again stunned into stillness as she stared at Charli, taking occasional glimpses at Gillian to make sure this was no parlor trick.

Finally Charli spoke. "Why did you give me away?" she asked in a very small, little girl-like voice. Vulnerability and years of insecurity were clearly visible along with her uncanny likeness to Gillian.

Imelda took Charli's hand and they both sat on the bed. She looked from one daughter to the other. "You both *have* to believe me," she started, taking a deep breath, "I admit that I wasn't thrilled to be pregnant by your father and was desperate to get out of town. But I also didn't have *any* pre-natal care, so I had no idea that I was pregnant with twins. I remember taking a taxi to the hospital, because I was early and your father wasn't around, and I also remember be-ing given some drugs and getting a C-section. Later I was given only *one* child. Not two," she said adamantly. "I swear to God."

"This is not to say, given the person I was, that I wouldn't have given one away, but you have to believe me when I say that I didn't have that choice to make. Someone stole my baby." Tears began rolling down her cheek. She clasped her hand over her mouth and began to sob for the first time that Gillian could remember. "You are so beauti-ful," she finally said, hesitantly stroking Charli's cheek as though afraid she might break or disappear.

Charli searched her mother's eyes for the truth and saw it there before her. At the same time, they reached for each other, and then cried in each other's arms.

Gillian had never seen such raw, unrehearsed emotions from her mother and realized that no amount of acting in the world could come close to it. Watching her sister, who'd been through so much, finally have what she'd craved with-out even knowing it, touched her heart like nothing she'd ever experienced. She too was crying as mother and daugh-ter clung to each other, trying to make up for thirty years of missing love.

"I'm so sorry," Imelda repeated over and over, before

turning to Gillian. "I'm also sorry for not being the best mother to you, too. I know I've been self-centered and haven't always been there for you, even when we were phys-ically together. Please accept my apology."

The three women hugged each other for a long time, forming new bonds and healing old wounds.

Chapter 43

Since catching her mother and Max in bed together, Lauren had experienced an increasing feeling of fatigue and general malaise. Having suffered a bout of depression when she was married to Max, she dreaded the thought of it returning, but after Mildred was arrested for Paulette's murder it was all she could do just to get out of bed in the morning. Having Gideon around certainly helped, but she wondered if she'd ever feel as happy and carefree as she had before, when she and Gideon were on their own, far away from the drama of her dysfunctional family.

Now that Max and Mildred had both been arrested for the well-publicized murder of the celebrity publicist Paulette Dolliver, TV, radio, the Internet, print magazines, and newspapers were all taking part in a Sodom and Gomorrah-style feeding frenzy. The *New York Post,* in particular, was having a field day traipsing over the tattered remains of the Baines-Reynolds's family reputation.

Their raucous headlines read:

BAINES FAMILY HEIRESS SCREWS DAUGHTER,
KILLS NIECE TO KEEP SON-IN-LAW UNDER COVERS

DISGRACED HORNDOG ATTORNEY MAXIMILLIAN
NEUMAN III BEDDED WIFE'S MOTHER AND COUSIN,
THANKFULLY GRANDMOTHER ALREADY DECEASED

MURDERED PUBLICIST PAULETTE DOLLIVER
KILLED BY OWN AUNT, CRUELLA DE VILLE

COUGAR KILLS CUB TO KEEP TIGER IN HER TANK

Lauren couldn't bear to turn on the TV for fear of catching the ever-breaking news involving another sleazy aspect of the titillating murder case. Even the late-night crowd had gotten in on the action. Comedian and talk show host Conan O'Brien joked: "I heard today that Mildred Baines-Reynolds has started another chapter of Jack and Jill. It's called, Jack Does Jill, Jane, *and* Jackie."

Lauren was certain that her dignified grandmother was tossing and turning in her grave. Her poor father, Nathan, had simply left the country, and advised Lauren to do the same, but she could barely muster the energy to get out of bed, let alone dress and pack.

"Everything's going to be okay," Gideon promised her. He brought in a tray of orange juice, fruit, and yogurt. Her appetite had been nonexistent lately and she was beginning to look pale and sallow.

"Things will never be okay," she said quietly, as she

stared at nothing in particular. She felt an overwhelming sense of doom. Everything she'd ever believed about herself and her family was one big fat lie, leaving her with nothing but an empty shell.

"Lauren, you've got to eat," Gideon insisted. He spooned a little yogurt and tried feeding it to her himself. She simply turned her head, refusing to eat. She'd been lying there wasting away for four days, not answering her phone, eating, or venturing out of the hotel room. He was beginning to be seriously alarmed.

The hotel room phone rang and Gideon picked it up. "Hello?"

"May I speak to Ms. Reynolds, please?" a male voice asked.

"May I ask who's calling?" Gideon inquired. Of course, the media had gotten wind of the fact that they were staying at the Gansevoort and had tried every trick in the book to get a comment or photo. One desperate reporter even claimed to be from maintenance sent to check for a carbon monoxide leak.

"This is Dr. Harris. I've been trying reach Lauren for days now. It's important that I speak to her."

Alarmed, Gideon left the room to try and figure out what was going on before causing Lauren any more concern. "Is everything okay?" he whispered, suddenly remembering that Lauren had been planning to get her annual checkups while in New York and getting scared. He wasn't sure that she could take any more bad news.

"I'm sorry, to whom am I speaking?" the doctor asked.

"I'm Lauren's boyfriend, Gideon."

"I'm sorry, Gideon, but I'm not allowed, because of client-patient confidentiality, to disclose Lauren's medical information without her consent."

"If you'll wait just a moment, I'll put her on the phone." Gideon took a deep breath, said a silent prayer, and walked back into the bedroom.

"Honey, Dr. Harris is on the line for you." He reluctantly handed her the phone.

Concern settled across the mask of despair that had etched itself onto Lauren's normally radiant face. "What is it?" She'd forgotten about her doctor's visits. For her they were simply a routine matter she took care of at the beginning of every year. It never dawned on her that anything could really be wrong with her.

"I'm sorry, honey, but he won't tell me, only you." He only wished that he could handle whatever it was and protect Lauren from any further hurt.

Lauren looked at the phone as though it were a venomous snake. "Hello?" she answered tentatively.

"Hi, Lauren, this is Dr. Harris. I've tried calling your cell with no luck, so I had Rachelle track down your hotel."

"Hi, Dr. Harris. I'm sorry. I completely forgot that I was supposed to call for my test results. Is everything okay?" she asked, her heart skipping several beats.

Gideon watched Lauren closely, as he held his breath. He couldn't bear the thought of something else happening to Lauren. She had certainly been through enough the last three years. He only wished that he could get his hands on

Max to give him the ass kicking he so richly deserved. Gideon watched anxiously as Lauren's face transformed from concern, to disbelief, to shock.

"Thank you, Dr. Harris. I'll call later to schedule a follow up."

Lauren hung up the phone and hugged Gideon for dear life. Her eyes were closed and he could feel her hot tears streaming down his neck.

"Baby, is everything okay?" he asked, frightened.

She finally got a handle on herself, pulled away from him, and wiped away the tears. "Everything is fine."

"Then why are you crying?"

"This time they're tears of joy," she said, as a smile lit up her face. "I'm pregnant!"

Chapter 44

"He sang like Tweety Bird," Gillian said.

Reese sat across the cafeteria table from her looking dumbfounded. "I still can't believe that Max and Lauren's mom, who I'd always thought was more pure than Claire Huxtable, were getting it on, and then plotted to kill Paulette." Reese felt as if she'd woken up lost in the twilight zone when Gillian told her the complete Max story.

"I'm just glad that he agreed to be tested for Rowe."

"So am I," Reese said. Her relief surpassed all of her fears. She no longer worried how she'd make ends meet without Chris's monthly check. It didn't matter. She'd sell the house, her cars, and clean her own toilets, if only her son could be healed.

"You know, he always did want a child. Remember how he'd pressed Lauren to get pregnant?"

"Yeah, I guess he just didn't want one by Paulette."

"Obviously, but let's be clear, Max is only doing this

hoping for some leniency with his charges and sentencing. Remember he is a lawyer."

"Or, *was* a lawyer."

"True that."

"Did you tell Lauren about me and Max?" Reese asked.

"Yes, I did. Given the circumstances, I had to in order to have the authorities press Max to be tested."

"What did she say?"

"After everything that she's been through because of Max and his indiscretions, I hate to disappoint you, but yours ranked pretty low on the list."

"I hope she can forgive me."

"If I were you I wouldn't worry about it. Her main concern is that Rowe gets his transplant."

"I'm so thankful for friends like you guys. I don't know if I always deserve you."

"Don't be so hard on yourself."

Just then Dr. Young appeared at the table, seemingly out of breath.

Reese's heart nearly stopped, knowing that this was Rowe's last chance. His condition had been worsening by the day, and Dr. Young didn't expect that he'd be strong enough to hang on long enough to wait for a donor from the national bank.

She rallied what strength she had left and stood up to face the man who she prayed would save her son.

"The tests just came back—"

"And?"

"It's a near perfect match." The smile that spread across

his face was one that Reese hadn't seen since the whole ordeal began.

Without thinking, she leapt into his arms. "Thank you, thank you, thank you," she said in between a flurry of kisses that she planted all over his face.

Gillian stood as well and hugged them both. Knowing that there was hope for Rowe proved to be so much more important than Internet photos, Oscar awards, or fame and fortune.

"Whoa, if I'd known I'd get this kind of attention, I'd have tracked Max down myself," he teased. "But let's not pop the cork yet, we've got to get through the transplant and pray that it takes."

For the first time, Reese wasn't worried. She felt certain that her prayers were being heard and that her son would be just fine.

Chapter 45

With the Academy Awards show less than two weeks away, the jockeying for position between the nominees, studios, and handlers had reached a fevered pitch. A couple of the actresses in Gillian's category had even gone to the extent of painting themselves as anointed saints by quickly affiliating with charities promoting teen abstinence and decrying pornography. In other words, contrasting themselves to the unscrupulous harlot Gillian Tillman-Russell. These were the big leagues and it was necessary to get rid of one's competition any way possible.

Besides, no one believed Gillian's feeble protestations of innocence. Her very own people, including those bought and paid for by the studios or Brandon's own deep pockets, couldn't prove that the photos were doctored. Yet, she somehow expected Joe and Jane Public, as well as the voting members of the Academy, to believe that she wasn't the star of those raunchy, degrading pictures.

Over three hundred journalists were now gathered in a

ballroom at the Four Seasons in Beverly Hills for a press conference that promised to address the ever-growing archive of salacious photos that had effectively torpedoed any chances Gillian had of taking home that highly coveted little gold statue. They stood twenty deep like a pack of wild, ravenous dogs, teeth bared, hungry for flesh, waiting to be served up what was left of Gillian Tillman-Russell's battered reputation.

CoAnne approached the microphone and said, "Thanks for coming this afternoon. I have a brief statement to make, which you will receive copies of, and then I'll take questions."

"As you all know, earlier this week Maximillian Neuman was arrested for the murder of Paulette Dolliver. During the course of that investigation it was revealed that he was also the person responsible for the pictures that have been widely circulated and falsely reported to be Gillian Russell."

From the back of the room, someone shouted, "Are you saying they were doctored?"

"No, I—"

Another reporter who was anxious for the next sound bite interrupted her. "So are you finally admitting that Gillian Russell did take those photos?"

"I didn't say that," CoAnne countered.

"How could the photos be real, and not be Gillian?" another voice demanded.

"While the pictures were not doctored, they were also *not* pictures of Gillian."

"How could that be possible?" someone shouted from the back of the room.

"Because they were pictures of me," Charli said, stepping from backstage. While this was a hugely embarrassing confession for her to make, it was her idea to step forward in person in order to protect her sister from the harm that her selfish and ill-considered actions had caused.

The crowd stared in apparent, but unspoken, confusion, until a woman finally yelled out to CoAnne, "What are you all trying to pull? We all know that's Gillian."

"No, *I'm* Gillian." When the real Gillian stepped from backstage and stood next to her twin, an audible gasp filled the room and dozens of flashbulbs lit up like flickering fireflies.

CoAnne turned to the audience and said, "I'd like to introduce you to Gillian's identical twin sister, Charli."

The room erupted in mayhem as every reporter present tried to ask questions at the same time.

"Who are you?" a woman asked, shoving her microphone forward.

"Where did you come from?" another one asked.

"Gillian, did you know about her?"

"Are you an actress, too?"

"How do you know Max?"

"Is this all a big publicity stunt?"

"Please, may I have your attention," CoAnne shouted above the noise. "Gillian, had no knowledge of Charli's existence until just this week, so she was just as puzzled as the rest of us about the pictures that were released," she explained. "Max met Charli in Atlanta and manipulated her into staging those shots. I'm also at liberty to tell you—

thanks to Gillian's efforts—police detectives were able to obtain a confession from Max for Paulette's murder. So not only is Gillian innocent of posing for the pictures we've all seen, she is also being heralded as a hero by police departments in Los Angeles, New York, and Atlanta for her assistance in solving the death of the celebrity publicist who was also once her dear friend."

A new round of shots caught pictures of Gillian and Charli side by side, as reporters began formulating the next hour's, or day's, headlines, which would immediately transform Gillian from a whoring, sleazy tramp to Nancy Drew in Manolos.

Afterward CoAnne, Gillian, Charli, Brandon, and Imelda sat watching the unfurling of the spin the media now placed on the whole debacle. The press was not only redeeming, it was gushing in its praise for Gillian's bravery and grace at handling the torturous scandal.

"Well, I think you may have done it," Brandon said to CoAnne.

"I didn't do anything. We're just lucky that Gillian and Lauren figured it out, and that Charli was willing to step forward."

"I'd do anything for my sister," she said, looking at Gillian adoringly. Her new relationship with Gillian was effortless, and her relationship with her mother was also developing nicely.

"Not that it really matters, but do you think the press will believe that I didn't realize that Charli existed?" Imelda asked.

"I think it helps now that the sheriff's investigation has uncovered other instances around the same time and vicinity of babies being stolen and sold illegally."

Apparently the local doctor and a noble minister's wife, who was a friend of Charli's adoptive mother's, were adept at talking vulnerable young girls out of their children, then selling them for profit. So when Imelda came along, only expecting one child and not too thrilled about that one, and without family present, it was the perfect opportunity to take the other twin while she was sedated and sell her to out-of-town clients, which is exactly what they did.

"No matter how it happened, I'm just glad that we're all together now," Imelda said, embracing her daughters. For the first time in her life she felt content with where she was at this very moment and didn't feel compelled to scheme and connive to reach the next one. Right here, right now was more than good enough for her.

Chapter 46

"So the King has come down from the Hollywood Hills to grace the little people with his presence," Tyrone said. His voice was deep and thick with sarcasm. Brandon hadn't been back to Mississippi since he left decades ago, and his discomfort at sitting in a room that had been badly decorated in the seventies was starkly apparent. He would rather have been getting a root canal, followed by a prostate exam, than be here. He thought long and hard about whether to walk into the lion's den, but realized that he didn't have a choice.

"We need to talk," Brandon said, taking a seat and accepting a shot of what could have been moonshine, or arsenic, from Tyrone's henchman, Two Tons.

Unless Brandon freed himself from ties to organized crime, he'd never be able to enjoy the life that he'd worked so hard to build, and he certainly wouldn't be able to do it with Gillian. He only hoped that it wasn't too late for them to have a fresh start.

He now realized that initially he'd loved Gillian mainly for her beauty and allure, but now he truly loved the whole person and prayed that she felt the same way about him. He also realized that when they married she wasn't truly in love with him either, and he regretted that he'd put her in the position of making an unfair choice between her dreams, which he was prepared to make reality, and her heart. He now realized that the two were inextricably connected.

"What can I do for you?" Tyrone asked. Today he wore a leopard print smoking jacket and matching slippers. His hair was freshly permed and pin-curled.

"I want out," Brandon said, simply.

"But you just got here," Tyrone said, showing a grille of gold teeth in what was meant as a smile.

Brandon smirked, realizing that Tyrone was not going to make this easy. "You know what I mean. It's time that we end our relationship. I can't do this anymore."

"But I thought we were friends," Tyrone said, feigning a sad expression.

"Let's be honest, we've never been friends," Brandon said, crossing his legs. "This was a relationship that suited us both at different times, but those days are over. It's time to move on."

Tyrone eyed Two Tons, who stood guard near the door. "It's not over till I say it's over," he growled, standing up to confront Brandon. Physically imposing Two Tons closed in on him from the other side.

Though fear rose to the surface, Brandon never showed it, realizing how true it was that animals could smell fear and would act accordingly and that Tyrone's barbarian acts of violence and revenge were legendary. Brandon uncrossed his legs and stood to face the gangster, toe-to-toe. He didn't flinch. "I'm prepared to settle this on amicable terms, but I do intend to settle it. It doesn't do either of us any good to continue our relationship given the media scrutiny that I've been under and will continue to be under. So we can part ways while we're both still intact or we can keep gambling until our luck runs out, and I'm not prepared to keep gambling."

This was hard to hear for a man who was accustomed to calling the shots. "If it weren't for me you'd still be selling bootleg tapes on the corner, right down the street from here."

"That may be true, but in any case, you've been adequately compensated for that over the years." Brandon had laundered many millions of dollars through Sound Entertainment on Tyrone's behalf, and since it had been sold he was now being pressured to run even more drug money through his film production company. So far, he'd come up with excuses to delay doing so, realizing that the first time he did it, he'd be back on the hook for another decade.

"I don't agree."

"So what do you want?" Brandon came prepared to negotiate.

While Tyrone paced the room, deep in thought, Brandon braced himself for some extreme demand of money; instead, to his surprise Tyrone said, "Have you met my son?"

"Junior? Yeah," Brandon answered, now truly confused.

What did a gangster's twenty-three-year-old son have to do with anything?

"He wants to be an actor. And he can sing, too." The menace had left Tyrone's voice and was replaced by an anxious excitement.

Brandon was nearly speechless. He was prepared to negotiate hard for his freedom, to risk his life if necessary. In fact, he'd considered doing a deal with the feds and flipping on Tyrone but realized that being beholden to the feds could be worse than his affiliation with any gangster. Then he'd thought about buying them off once and for all, but realized that he would only be giving them more fodder for blackmail and allowing them to sink their clutches even deeper into his hide. After years of hand-wringing and gut wrenching who knew that all he had to do was put Junior in a movie?

"Junior, come on in here!" Tyrone shouted over his shoulder.

Seconds later an overweight young man shuffled into the room wearing baggy pants with his head hung low.

"You want to be in the movies, right?"

"Yeah," he mumbled.

"This here is Brandon Russell, you know, married to Gillian Tillman-Russell, the big movie star. Well, he gon' put you in da movies. Right, Brandon?"

"Absolutely." Brandon didn't care if Junior could carry a tune in a bucket or utter another word besides the one he'd just spoken; he was going to be in the movies!

Tyrone looked like he had just won the lottery. "You hear that, Junior, you're gonna be in the movies!"

Brandon stood up and shook Tyrone's hand. "So, we cool, right?"

"We cool," Tyrone said. He walked over to a velvet picture of Isaac Hayes that concealed a hidden safe. After dialing the combination he pulled out the flash drive and handed it to Tyrone.

"This is yours, and it's the only copy," he said, turning the evidence over to Brandon.

Later, as his plush private jet took off, soaring over the Delta, Brandon felt as if he could fly himself. After years of being choked by his ties to the underworld he was finally free.

Chapter 47

The Russell estate was beautifully deco-
rated for the fabulous pre-Oscar party in honor of Gillian's
nomination. It was three days before the big awards ceremony and the Who's Who of both the film and music in-
dustries were on hand to share the moment with this year's
golden girl. Win, lose, or draw, Gillian was the reigning "It"
Girl of Hollywood after being cleared of the scurrilous
accusations surrounding the pornographic pictures that
nearly wrecked her career and helping to arrest the accused
killer of one of their own, celebrity publicist Paulette
Dolliver.

Tuxedo-clad waiters passed trays of vintage Krug to
over one hundred well-dressed movers and shakers, along
with sumptuous delicacies, such as caviar pâté, sautéed sea
scallops, and grilled figs stuffed with goat cheese and
wrapped in Spanish prosciutto. While a fifty-piece orchestra
played, the crowd was soothed and stimulated by the smooth
vocals of Jennifer Freeman. Brandon had spared no expense

to celebrate his wife's success. He had never been more proud of her than he was right now.

When Gillian began her descent down the grand marble staircase into the Gothic ballroom, the elite crowd burst into rousing applause. She looked regal wearing a chartreuse Anna Sui sheath dress and poised beyond her years. Her twin sister, Charli, wearing an elegant Narciso Rodriguez pantsuit, stood next to, Imelda, both beaming with pride. For the first time in her life, Imelda wasn't interested in seeking the spotlight herself. She simply relished her daughter's big moment. And Charli felt as if her life was just beginning; CoAnne had arranged for her and Gillian to also meet their father.

Lauren and Gideon stood at the foot of the staircase waiting to greet Gillian with hugs and kisses. As a waiter passed by, Gillian accepted a glass of Champagne and handed one to Gideon and Lauren, who politely declined.

"How are we supposed to celebrate with no Champagne?" Gillian beamed. She was caught up in the moment but wanted to steal a little private time with her best friend before the rest of the crowd surrounded her.

"I'll just have to do it with San Pellegrino instead," Lauren answered. She, too, was beaming, but for a much different reason.

"Since when have you ever turned down Champagne?" Gillian asked, remembering the Champagne-fueled nights they used to share with Reese and Paulette. "This is vintage Krug. You know my husband—only the best."

"Since I found out that *my* husband and I are having a baby."

Gillian shook her head as if to clear it to be sure of what she'd heard. "Husband? Baby? What are you talking about?"

Lauren and Gideon both laughed. They'd secretly got hitched the day before and Gillian was the first person they'd told about the marriage or about Lauren's pregnancy. "We got married yesterday, and yes, we are having a baby!"

Gillian had never seen Lauren so happy. She knew that her mother's betrayal and arrest had caused Lauren great pain, but thankfully the joy of her new family seemed to have soothed some of the heartache.

"Oh my God! Congratulations! I'm so excited!" she screamed.

"What's going on here?" Reese walked over to the three-some and hugged everyone but lingered when she embraced Lauren. "I'm so sorry for what happened. Would you please forgive me?" Even though Rowe's bone marrow transplant was scheduled for the next morning, Reese felt that she had to come out tonight to support Gillian, who had always been there for her.

"Consider it done," Lauren said with a very broad smile. Nothing could steal her joy at this moment.

"So, what *is* going on here?" Reese asked again, looking around at all of the smiling faces.

"We're having a baby!" Lauren blurted out.

"When did all of this happen?" Reese asked, hugging Lauren.

"It's a long but very happy story," Lauren answered.

"Well, you deserve every bit of it," Reese said. She'd always been a little jealous of Lauren. She envied the fact that she'd been born into wealth and privilege and came with a pedigree that she never had to strive to achieve. In addition to all of that, she was also drop-dead gorgeous. It had all seemed unfair to Reese, who'd had to scheme, scrape, and fight for everything she'd ever had. But over the last few years, and especially within the last week, she'd come to realize that the grass is always greener and much more plush on the other side of the street, even if the street was in Beverly Hills. What she truly admired was the grace with which Lauren handled both sides. It was time that she found some of that grace. After all, she, too, was blessed in so many ways.

"Thank you," Lauren said, smiling from ear to ear.

Gideon took a glass of sparking water from a passing waiter for Lauren, and Gillian raised her glass of Champagne. "I'd like to propose a toast to the missing member of our foursome, Paulette. If it weren't for her generosity, I wouldn't be here, so I'd like to dedicate this night to our sister." They each raised their glasses in honor of Paulette.

Just then the band quieted down and Brandon took the stage and motioned for Gillian to join him. He looked fabulous in a custom Armani tuxedo. Gillian also noticed that he seemed more settled and confident than she'd ever known him to be.

"Thank you all for coming out to celebrate my wife, Gillian's, Oscar nomination," he began.

The room burst into spontaneous applause.

Brandon looked at Gillian beaming with pride and said, "My wife is the most beautiful and most talented—"

"Bitch!" a near-hysterical sounding voice boomed.

Everyone turned to see a woman standing—though swaying slightly—in the back of the room with a glazed, drug-induced haze in her eyes. It was Lydia, who had managed to sneak onto the property, seeking revenge. Since being forced to cancel her book, her publisher was demanding repayment of the hefty advance—much of which she'd already spent—her ex-fiancé had reneged on his re-proposal, and she was now the laughingstock of Hollywood. No amount of therapy, cocaine, or barbiturates could soothe the anger that she felt.

Security began moving in her direction, but before they could get to her, she pulled a pistol from her shoulder bag and began waving it around erratically. Her hands were shaking as she yelled, "Don't come any closer, or I'll shoot."

"Lydia, put the gun down," Brandon said in a calm, even voice.

"Don't you tell me what to do!" she screamed. "I did everything for your precious Gillian, and what did you do? You fired me! Threw me away like trash."

"Lydia, I'm sorry," he said in his most soothing voice, trying to calm her down and keep her attention on him until one of the security guards was able to sneak up on her.

"I'll bet you're sorry," she spat bitterly. "I put everything I had into making Gillian a star and you fired me because of her gold-digging, has-been mother? Then you send your goons after me."

"Lydia, I didn't send anyone after you."

"You're a liar!" she screamed. "And I have proof." She pulled a note from her pocket and shook it at him.

It was Paulette's note, Brandon realized. "Lydia, calm down."

"Fuck you and your golden girl," she said, aiming the gun at Gillian.

Just then, one of the security guards lunged at her, grabbing for the gun.

Everyone screamed.

But it was too late.

She'd pulled the trigger.

A bullet went flying toward its target.

Chapter 48

The mood in the ER waiting room at Cedars-Sinai was one of gloom and doom. The bullet, a .38 caliber, had punctured a lung, but thanks to the paramedics, the patient made it to Cedars-Sinai's emergency room with a steady though weak pulse.

Brandon, Lauren, and Reese huddled together, each saying silent prayers that she would pull through.

The surgeon on call, Dr. Edmonds, approached the group wearing a somber expression of his own. "You can visit her, but not for long and only one at a time."

"How is she?" Brandon asked anxiously.

"She's still alive, which is a miracle considering the internal damage, but it is touch and go."

"Brandon, you should hurry," Reese said.

When he entered the intensive care room, he nearly froze in his steps at the sight before him.

"Tell me she'll be okay," Gillian begged, tears streaming

down her face, taking with them all traces of the glamorous Academy Award–nominated actress from the previous night. At this moment, she was simply a daughter distraught over the possibility of losing her mother; a mother whom she'd never completely understood. And after the brave and self-less act of jumping between a bullet and Gillian, she understood her even less. One thing was clear though, for the first time, Gillian felt as if her mother truly did love her.

Brandon held Gillian while together with Charli they watched Imelda clinging to life. Her once beautiful face was gaunt and drained of color. She appeared thirty years older, Gillian thought.

"Imelda is tough, remember that. If anybody can pull through this, she can," Brandon said.

Suddenly, the rhythmic hum of machines turned to a frantic chaotic burst of warnings, and seconds later a team of doctors and nurses rushed into the room shoving Gillian and Brandon aside in their frantic attempt to keep Imelda from flatlining.

Shock set in as Gillian faced that harsh reality that she could lose her mother before ever having the chance to thank her for saving her life.

It was all a blur. She remembered standing by as Brandon spoke and then registering some commotion in the crowd and seeing a deranged-looking Lydia emerge from the crowd. The next thing she knew, there was a loud sound and Imelda lurched forward to cover her, knocking them both to the ground. When the chaos subsided, there was a crowd around the two of them and her mother wasn't moving.

Blood pooled beneath her. She and Charli screamed at the same time.

Later in the waiting room, Reese sat holding Charli's hands, while they waited for the doctors to stabilize her mother.

"Let's pray," Reese said. Rowe and Max had just been taken into surgery and she felt compelled to try yet another prayer, not only for Rowe, but also for Imelda, whom she now had a much greater level of respect for after she risked her own life to save her daughter's. If Imelda could be redeemed as a mother, it gave Reese hope that so could she.

Charli looked at her as though she were a bit surprised. From what little she knew about Reese, she didn't seem to be the praying kind, but she bowed her head nonetheless.

"Dear God, we come before you as weak, and sometimes unworthy subjects, but awed by your power and made better by your greatness. Also, knowing that until our last breath, it's never too late to learn how to walk the path through which you guide us. Though I've never fully understood your role in my life, I now know that you *are* my life, and that I am your manifestation on earth. In your son, Jesus Christ's name, I pray to you for understanding and for mercy for both friends and fauxs. I also pray for healing. I pray that you will heal our hearts and our minds and our bodies. In particular I pray for your child, my son, Rowe Nolan, as he prepares for his transplant, and most urgently, I pray for your daughter, and Gillian and Charli's mother,

Imelda, as she fights for the life that you've blessed us with. In Jesus' name, I pray. Amen."

When Reese opened her eyes and held her head up, there stood Chris.

"When did you find religion?" he asked, looking skeptical.

"I didn't," she said softly, "it found me."

"I'm glad to hear that," Chris said.

"What are you doing here?" Reese hadn't heard from Chris since he stormed out of the house, only from his lawyers. They'd phoned threatening to discontinue child support payments. At first she was petrified at the thought of losing the money that she relied on to pay all of her bills. The remainder of her lump-sum settlement, what she hadn't put in the house and spent on material things, had shrunk considerably with the slump on Wall Street. She soon realized that as long as she and Rowe had their health, their friends, and each other, the rest really didn't matter as much as she'd always thought it did.

"I'm here for Rowe."

Her face twisted in confusion. "But you walked out?" She didn't expect to ever see him again, unless it was in court.

"Yes, I did, because I was angry at you, but that has nothing to do with Rowe. He may not be my biological son, but I still love him, and I'll always be here for him."

Brandon raced over and called to Charli, "You should come in now, it doesn't look good."

The alarm on Brandon's face made her blood run cold. She was just coming to terms with losing the woman she'd always thought was her mother, but to find her real mom and lose her in the same week was unbearable.

She and Brandon raced down the hall into the intensive care room where the trauma team had managed to restart Imelda's heart, but she was still unconscious and her vitals were sketchy.

Gillian and Charli hugged, clinging to each other and to the fading hope that they would not lose their mother. After wiping their tears, they each stood on one side of the bed, holding one of Imelda's perfectly manicured hands.

"Mom, can you hear me?" Gillian asked. "Charli and I are both here with you. Everything is going to be okay."

"Yes, Mom. Gillian is right. You're gonna be fine," Charli said, though her fresh stream of tears said otherwise.

"Mom, you have to wake up, we need you and we love you." Gillian realized she'd never told her mom that she loved her, which brought a fresh stream of tears down her cheeks as well. "I love you so much."

At that moment Imelda stirred, tightening her weak grip on both their hands.

Gillian turned to Brandon. "Go get the doctor, I think she's waking up."

In seconds Dr. Edmonds was taking vitals and increasing meds. "She appears a lot more stable, her blood pressure is up, and her heartbeat is stronger."

A sense of relief washed over Gillian and Charli when they saw their mother's eyes flicker open.

"Mom, it's us, Gillian and Charli," Gillian said anxiously. Tears of joy began to flow. "We thought we were losing you."

"You . . . think . . . I'd . . . miss . . . the . . . Oscars?" she managed weakly, before she closed her eyes again to rest.

Gillian turned to Charli, smiled, and said, "I think she's going to be just fine."

Chapter 49

After months of hype, hyperventilation, and much speculation, the big day had finally arrived. Tinseltown was abuzz with gossip and chatter about what designers celebrities were wearing as they inched ever so slowly down the red carpet, pretending to avoid being stopped along the way for those syrupy and sometimes catty interviews with *E!, Access Hollywood,* and anybody else with a cameraman, a live mic, and a talking head.

Between the truckloads of diamonds, flashy designer gowns, exfoliated, Botoxed, self-tanned, and professionally made-up faces, the Kodak Theatre felt more like a three-ring circus with too many ringmasters than an auditorium.

Gillian Tillman-Russell wore a gray warm-up suit by Juicy Couture, brown and gray sneakers by Nike, and dark circles under her eyes. The style was completed by the bedhead grunge look, but no one in her entourage cared the least.

"You don't wish you were there?" Charli asked her.

Gillian, Charli, Brandon, Reese, Chris, Lauren, and Gideon were all seated in a large hospital room along with both Rowe and Imelda. The hospital had thrown together an impromptu Oscar party. A large flat-screen TV hung on the wall so they could watch the Academy Awards to see if Gillian would win the ever-prestigious Oscar.

"There is no other place in the world that I'd rather be," Gillian answered. Though she'd fantasized for months about walking the red carpet and being among the glitterati of Hollywood, fantasyland was quickly put into perspective by the reality of nearly losing her mother and of Reese nearly losing her son.

"I wish I could say the same thing," Imelda retorted. Though she was still weak, she was back to being herself, having ordered a hair stylist to come to her hospital room, diva style, insisting that she'd feel much better much quicker if only her hair were done. The next call was for a manicure and pedicure.

Reese laughed. "There was a time when I would have moved the heavens, the Earth, *and* Gillian aside to be there, but I agree, there is no other place in the world I'd rather be than right here." She reached over and rubbed Rowe's cheek, which now actually had a little color in it. The bone marrow transplant had gone beautifully and there was already an improvement in his white blood count.

"I'd rather be playing soccer," he said with a little smirk. The active little boy that they knew before was making a comeback.

"Soon, little man, soon," Chris said, rubbing his head.

He didn't care who his biological father was, Rowe was *his* son, and that was all that mattered. Max, selfish as always, had no desire to get involved in Rowe's life, and only donated the bone marrow to get a more favorable sentence for his involvement in Paulette's death.

Reese turned to Lauren and smiled. "Soon you'll have your own little one to love and worry about."

"I know. We couldn't be happier about it. I'm just sorry that my mom won't be around to experience it with me." Having her mother, who was out on bail, charged with murder was still more like a Hollywood drama than anything that could have happened in her life. Though Mildred had called Lauren repeatedly, Lauren wasn't ready to face the ugliness of her mother and her actions. But she was ready to get on with her life. She and Gideon had decided to cut down on their world travel until after the baby was born. In the meantime, they were opening galleries in both New York and L.A. so Lauren would be closer to her friends, who were now more like her family.

"Shhh, shhhh," Imelda said, "the best actress category is coming up."

They all grew quiet, as Jennifer Hudson walked forward to present the award.

After reciting the nominees and showing glowing clips of each performance, she said, "And the winner is . . . Gillian Tillman-Russell!"

The hospital room erupted, and all who could jumped up and ran over to hug Gillian, who stood still in shock.

Though she'd imagined winning, she never really believed that she would.

"Gillian Russell isn't here to accept her award, as you all know; her mother, Baroness Imelda von Glich, is still in the hospital recuperating."

"She mentioned my name! She mentioned my name!" squealed Imelda, who was now feeling even better. A couple of networks had already called to interview her about her heroism. Larry King had even called. She couldn't wait to get out of the hospital to hit the circuit. Maybe she should get her own publicist . . .

"So I'll accept the award on her behalf. Congratulations, Gillian!"

"Yeah, congratulations, baby. You deserve it," Brandon said, hugging her close. "And I love you, and always will." He could barely contain his happiness; Imelda and Rowe were alive and well, Gillian had won the little gold statue, and he'd managed to remove Paulette's note from Lydia's mad clutches after security took her down. Suitcase finally closed.

"I love you, too," Gillian said, and for the first time since she'd known Brandon, she *really* meant it.

Epilogue

"Awww, she is so adorable!" Gillian said, smooching the cute little two-month-old's chubby cheeks.

"I'm already claiming her for Rowe," Reese said. "She is a beauty!"

"Thank you," Lauren said, beaming with pride at her gorgeous, healthy, and happy baby girl. "But you'll have to talk to Gideon, I don't think he'll *ever* want her to date."

"Isn't that right, daddy's little girl," she cooed.

"Thanks, guys, for coming to New York and all the way up here to Westchester, but I know that this is what Paulette would want."

"Which Paulette?" Gillian teased.

In honor of her cousin, Lauren named her daughter Paulette. They'd gathered at her graveside to celebrate Paulette Dolliver's life and to introduce her to her new little cousin, Paulette Gimble.

Reese popped the cork on a bottle of Paul Goerg, Paulette's favorite Champagne, and filled their glasses with the bubbly elixir.

They all raised their flutes high to the sky, and Lauren sang out, "To you, Paulette. May you finally rest in peace."

Readers' Guide

1. Did Reese's initial decision to put other things ahead of Rowe's life necessarily mean that she didn't love him?

2. Do you think Lydia was mentally disturbed from the beginning, or was she driven past the brink by fame, fortune, and too much cocaine? Do you blame her for wanting to get back at Gillian, Brandon, and Imelda for the way they fired her "unjustly," ruining her career?

3. Was Lauren truly happy globe-trotting with Gideon, or was she, once again, simply running away from reality and keeping her head buried in the sand? Do you think that her and Gideon's relationship will last? Why or why not?

4. Is Imelda any different from many parents who give birth expecting that their children will take care of them in old age?

5. Do you feel that Imelda's lessons have been truly learned at the end? Do you think she is a changed person? Or do you think she will just revert back to her old ways, using Gillian for her fame and fortune? Explain.

6. Do you think Charli was fully responsible for her life as a stripper, or were her poor circumstances responsible, giving her no other choice?

7. Should Dr. Young have gone ahead and told Chris that he wasn't Rowe's father—when Reese didn't—in order to get to the real father more quickly? Do you think that, in a situation where a life is on the line, a doctor has the right to disregard a patient's privacy and interfere with family affairs?

8. Between Mildred and Max, who most used whom? Explain.

9. Do you think that Chris will continue to support Rowe and Reese financially after finding out that he is not Reese's biological father? Should he?

10. Even though Charli and Gillian are identical twins, should Brandon have believed his wife when she told him that the pornographic photos were not of her?

11. Between Gillian and Brandon, who is most to blame for their dysfunctional relationship? Explain.

12. At the end, Gillian tells Brandon that she loves him and, for the first time, *really* means it. Do you think that all their problems are solved? Is there hope for Gillian and Brandon's relationship over the long term?

About the Author

Tracie Howard is the author of six books, including *Revenge Is Best Served Cold* (coauthored), *Why Sleeping Dogs Lie, Never Kiss and Tell, Gold Diggers,* and *Friends and Fauxs.* She is a former columnist and lifestyle editor for *Savoy* magazine, and a current contributor to *UpTown* magazine, among others. Tracie was recently a visiting professor at Institut Supérieure de Management in Senegal, Dakar. She is also co-owner of a fashion/lifestyle company called Ethos, and lives with her husband in Atlanta, Georgia.